Sunny Boy in the Big City

Ramy Allison White

Illustrated by Charles L. Wrenn

Sunny Boy was speaking to the tall policeman who directed traffic from the center of the street.

SUNNY BOY
IN THE BIG CITY

BY

RAMY ALLISON WHITE

Author of
"Sunny Boy in the Country," "Sunny
Boy at the Seashore," etc.

ILLUSTRATED BY

CHARLES L. WRENN

1920

CONTENTS

ILLUSTRATIONS

CHAPTER I
THE PARADE

"**F**all in!" said Sunny Boy sharply.

The army, six small boys distributed comfortably over the front steps, scrambled to obey. That is, all except one, who remained seated, a sea shell held over each ear.

"I said 'Fall in,'" repeated Sunny Boy patiently, as a general should speak.

"I heard you the first time," admitted the small soldier. "Did you know these shells made a noise, Sunny?"

"Of course," answered Sunny Boy scornfully. "Any shell sounds like that if you hold it up to your ear. Come on, Bobbie, we're going to parade."

But Private Robert Henderson, it seemed, didn't feel like parading just that minute.

"Let's take this stuff out to the sand-box," he suggested. "We can make a real beach, with shells and everything. Gee, you must have had fun at the seashore."

"Did," said Sunny Boy briefly.

He was exasperated. As general of his army he tried not to be cross, but Bobbie was famous for always spoiling other people's plans. He never by any chance wanted to do what the other boys wanted to do.

"You can play with the sand-box after we parade," announced Sunny Boy now. "Come on, Bobbie."

Bobbie remained obstinately absorbed in the shells.

"Let me!" Down the steps tumbled a pink gingham frock and a fluff of yellow bobbed hair that proved to be four-year-old Ruth Baker.

1

She lived next door to Sunny Boy, and her brother, Nelson, was already marking time with the waiting army.

"Let me march, Sunny Boy," Ruth begged. "I can mark time, an' everything!"

Sunny Boy decided swiftly.

"All right," he assented. "I don't think much of girls in an army, but I s'pose it's better than being one short. Get in next to David."

Ruth's feelings were not easily hurt, and she didn't mind if her enlistment was not accepted with enthusiasm as long as she was accepted. She slipped happily into line back of David Spellman, a freckle-faced boy with smiling dark eyes.

"Forward, march!" Sunny Boy beat a lively quick-step on his drum and the army moved down the quiet street, leaving Bobbie Henderson playing with the shells.

Sunny Boy's drum, of all his toys, was probably his favorite. He had let it roll into the street once and a horse had nearly stepped on it, but his mother had mended it neatly with court-plaster, and it seemed good for many more days.

"Rub-a-dub, dub! Rub-a-dub, dub!" he pounded gaily now as he swung along at the head of his gallant forces.

"I don't think generals play drums," David Spellman had said doubtfully, when Sunny Boy first organized his army.

"Well, I'm going to play mine," Sunny Boy had retorted firmly. "Daddy says when you're short of help a man has to do two people's work. I can play my drum and be general, too."

"Halt!"

Sunny Boy issued his order so quickly that the army was startled and stepped on one another's heels as they came to a standstill.

"This square's a good place to drill," he explained. "I'll see how well you know the man'l of arms."

Sunny Boy meant the manual of arms, and his idea of army drill, gleaned from the talk of his father and one or two older cousins, wasn't very clear; but then, his army didn't know much about it either, so his authority wasn't questioned.

"Column right!" said Sunny Boy.

The army obediently turned to the right.

"Ruth, don't you know which is your right?" demanded Sunny Boy severely.

A general must keep up discipline, you know, and when a girl is in an army she must do just as the others do.

"I get mixed 'bout right and left," admitted Ruth Baker cheerfully. "But I'm all right now, Sunny. See?"

"All right," approved Sunny Boy graciously. "Column left!"

The army swung to the left.

"Look here, I don't intend to have you children making a noise like this in front of my house!" The handsome glass-paneled door of the house before which the army was drilling had opened suddenly. A woman whom Sunny Boy afterward described to his mother as "awful big and tall" came out on the steps and frowned down at the children. "Why on earth do all the children in the neighborhood pick out my house to play around?" she continued fretfully.

Sunny Boy's army wanted very much to run home, but he showed no signs of running himself so they waited, huddled together in a frightened little group.

"Why don't you stay at your own homes to play?" persisted the woman.

The woman really wasn't very tall, not taller than Sunny Boy's own mother. She came out so unexpectedly and stared down at the children so crossly that she seemed taller than she was. She had near-sighted eyes, and wore big, thick-rimmed glasses, and these, too, made her look more severe.

"Well?" she demanded.

Sunny Boy stood at the foot of the steps and smiled at her. He knew she wasn't always upset like this.

"You have such a nice sidewalk," he explained, putting down his drum and removing his cap as Mother had taught him. "It's so wide and smooth. I should think it would be great for roller-skating."

"I won't let 'em!" the woman answered quickly. "In the summer I just about spend my whole day chasing children off this walk. I didn't have it put down for a roller-skating rink. What are you young ones doing, anyhow?"

"This is my army," Sunny Boy indicated the column with a backward sweep of his hand. "We were marching, and we stopped to drill. But we'll go, if you'd rather."

"That's a cunning little girl," said the woman, looking at Ruth. "Is she a soldier, too? I thought only boys could join the army."

Sunny Boy explained that Ruth was taking the place of a private who didn't want to do his duty.

"We'll be going now," he added politely.

"Wait a minute," said the woman, who didn't seem cross at all now. "I've been bothered to death this morning—company telephoning they were coming to spend the afternoon and then changing their minds after I had the lemonade all made and on the ice. I have a lot to bother me."

She looked a little wistfully at Sunny Boy. He didn't know it, but she was trying to say she was sorry she had been impatient and testy. Grown-ups frequently find it as difficult to say "I'm sorry" as boys and girls do.

"I wonder if your army would like some nice ice-cold lemonade?" said the woman abruptly. "Would your mothers mind, do you think?"

"Not lemonade," Sunny Boy assured her promptly. "'Sides, it is a long time to lunch, and Mother doesn't mind if you don't eat just before lunch."

"Well, all right, then. But how shall I give it to you?" asked their would-be hostess. "If I bring it out here all the neighborhood will come and want some. And I do hate to have so many children tramping in over my clean rugs."

Not without reason was Sunny Boy a general.

"I can march 'em in the basement door," he suggested. "They'll stay in a row and not muss anything."

So it was decided. The woman went in and closed the door, promising to open the iron basement gate for them, and Sunny Boy turned to his army.

"Forward march!" he ordered.

A little fearfully the army marched down the area steps and into a dark hall. They each had a feeling that the woman might change her mind after all, and scold them again. But she was smiling as they tramped into her old-fashioned kitchen.

"Halt!" commanded Sunny Boy, and the army ranged itself against the wall without further orders.

"I'll give each one a glass, and then I'll pour the lemonade," said the hostess pleasantly.

She went down the line, filling a tall crystal glass for each child. Then, after that, she brought out a plate of brown and white cookies and insisted that they must each take three.

"Sugar cookies don't hurt any one," she declared, patting Ruth on the head as she passed her. "Do they, General?"

"I guess not," agreed Sunny Boy contentedly, munching a cake.

When they had finished, they put the glasses carefully on the table, and said "Thank you" politely.

"My name is Miss Lyons, Miss Edith Lyons," announced their hostess, following them to the door. "I'm going to watch you march off, and I hope you'll come to see me again."

"We didn't muss anything, did we?" asked Sunny Boy anxiously. He felt responsible for all the rest.

Miss Lyons stooped down and kissed him.

"Bless your heart, for a thoughtful little boy," she said warmly. "You haven't hurt a thing. Good-bye, Soldier, and good luck!"

"Fall in!" Sunny Boy commanded as they reached the walk. "Forward, march!"

The drum sounding merrily, the army fell into step and marched down the street, Miss Lyons waving her handkerchief in good-bye.

"Those were good cookies," chuckled Harold Wallace, who marched beside Sunny Boy. "Gee, I wanted to run when she opened the door. Did you know her, Sunny?"

"My, no," Sunny Boy assured him. "I guess she was just glad to have somebody come and drink up all that lemonade."

When they reached Sunny's house, a familiar touring car was drawn up at the curb.

"Daddy's home!" cried Sunny Boy. "P'haps he'll give us a ride. Where's Bobbie?"

Bobbie was not in sight, but his shells lay scattered on the top step where he had left them.

"Well, well, who wants a little ride?" Mr. Horton came smiling down the steps. "Sunny Boy, Mother wants you to pick up this stuff and put it in the hall. Any one's likely to fall over it out here. And then I'll take you round the park and back."

"All of us?" asked Sunny Boy, beginning to pick up the shells and sea-weed. "Where's Bobbie, Daddy?"

"All of you," assented Mr. Horton. "Bobbie Henderson? Oh, his mother sent for him. Ready now, children?"

Mr. Horton put Ruth Baker in the front seat because she was the only girl, and the seven boys piled happily into the tonneau. They were all ready to start when Sunny Boy, turning around, saw a grinning little colored boy holding on at the back of the car. Mr. Horton saw him, too.

"Hey, get down from there!" Sunny Boy's father called crisply. "You'll be hurt, taking a chance like that. Get off now, before I start the car."

The woolly black head and grinning brown face disappeared, but Sunny Boy set up a loud wail.

"Daddy, he took my hat! See him! He's got it! Let me get out and chase him!"

"Stay where you are," commanded Mr. Horton. "You can't catch him now. Perhaps we can find him later. If not, Mother will have to get you another hat to-morrow."

"It was brand-new," Sunny Boy explained mournfully to David, as the car started. "Mother bought it for me to wear to New York. And now that colored boy went and stole it!"

CHAPTER II
OLIVER'S LESSON

"Y ou going to New York?" Harold Wallace asked curiously. "When? My cousin lives there. He's coming to see me next summer."

Sunny Boy bounced around excitedly on the seat. That is, he bounced as much as he could in the rather crowded space.

"Yes, we're going to New York," he announced. "To-morrow—no, the next day—when is it, Daddy?"

"Soon," said Mr. Horton.

"Send me a post-card for my album," begged Ruth.

"Me, too," chimed in Nelson.

All the boys, it seemed, wanted post-cards from New York.

"Well, maybe, if Mother will write 'em," agreed Sunny Boy dubiously. "I can print A's and B's, but not a real letter writing. Are you going to get out, Daddy?"

The car had circled a large green that made attractive the center of the city, and Mr. Horton had parked before a busy grocery store.

"I'm going in here to do an errand for Mother," he said. "Now, youngsters, I won't be long, and every one of you stay in the car till I come back. I don't want to have to hunt up missing boys when it's time to go home."

Ruth Baker turned so she faced the back of the car.

"You never stay at home, Sunny Horton!" she declared accusingly. "I think it's mean. You were going to play Indian braves and sleep out in the tent, and pretty soon it will be so cold Mother won't let us."

"You have been away a lot, haven't you?" suggested David.

Sunny Boy considered.

"I had to go to see my Grandpa Horton," he urged. "And then I had to go to see my Aunt Bessie. And Daddy would be lonesome in New York without Mother and me. He said so."

You see, Sunny Boy had had a busy summer. First he and his mother had gone into the country to visit his grandfather who lived on a farm. Sunny Boy was named for this grandfather, "Arthur Bradford Horton," though Daddy and Mother called him Sunny Boy, and many people thought he had no other name. Grandfather Horton's farm was known as "Brookside," and Sunny Boy learned to love the place dearly in the month he spent there. You may have read what he did there and the friends he made in the first book about him, called "Sunny Boy in the Country."

After Sunny Boy and his mother came home from "Brookside," they went almost immediately to visit Mrs. Horton's sister, Sunny's Aunt Bessie, in her bungalow at Nestle Cove. Mr. Horton took them down to the seashore in the automobile, and Sunny Boy had a delightful time playing in the sand and learning to swim. He found a little lost dog, too, as you may remember if you have read the book about him called "Sunny Boy at the Seashore."

Now he was at home again in Centronia, the city where he and his daddy and mother lived, and they were getting ready to make a trip to the great city of New York.

"Where 'bouts does your cousin live?" Sunny Boy asked Harold Wallace, hoping his friends understood that all this traveling he was experiencing was truly necessary. "P'haps Mother and I'll see him."

"I don't know exactly where he lives," answered Harold cautiously. "But I know it is in a brick row. Aunt Lucy wrote my mother when they moved."

"I'll tell Daddy," promised Sunny Boy confidently. "He'll know what street. Don't get out, Oliver."

Oliver Dunlap, red-haired and blue-eyed, grinned provokingly.

"Wait till you see me," he retorted. "Can't I put just one foot out of the car?"

Of course, having one foot out, Oliver in another moment had both feet on the running board and from there jumped to the sidewalk.

"Daddy said to stay in the car," insisted Sunny Boy.

"He only meant not to go away," said Oliver. "Oh, look at the crowd coming!"

The children stood up in the car and stared in the direction Oliver was pointing. On the next block they could see a man running swiftly, followed by a crowd of people, and back of them two policemen.

"Come back, Oliver!" screamed Ruth, jumping up and down with excitement. "Make him come back, Sunny."

But before Oliver could run over to the car, if he had wanted to, the man, the crowd close upon his heels, had reached the spot where Oliver stood. He caught hold of him, whirled him about, and dropped something into his hands, all without stopping his headlong flight. The crowd immediately closed in around Oliver just as Mr. Horton, attracted by the noise and the shouting, came out of the store. One of the policemen continued to run after the man.

"Oh, Daddy, get Oliver," Sunny Boy almost sobbed, as his father came over to the car.

"Why, where is he?" asked Mr. Horton, surprised. "Aren't you all here?"

"Oliver isn't. He's in there." Sunny Boy pointed to the crowd which was growing larger every minute as more and more people pressed in, eager to know what the excitement was about. "Oh, gee!"

Sunny Boy's eyes grew wide with wonder and terror. The other boys in the car looked frightened. Ruth began to cry.

A policeman had come out from the center of the crowd, and he had Oliver by the arm. Oliver was crying, and looked very small and miserable.

"Why, Oliver Dunlap!" Mr. Horton walked up to him, and put his arm protectingly around the frightened child. "What is the matter, Officer?"

"Do you know him?" asked the policeman politely. "Maybe that's different then. That pickpocket stole a lady's purse, and here's the empty bag he left in the kid's hands. We thought they were together—using the boy to cover up his tracks, you see."

"I left him in my car ten minutes ago with these other children," said Mr. Horton calmly. "He's Henry Dunlap's son. Your chief knows his father."

"If you say it's all right, it is," pronounced the policeman. "Don't cry, kid, you're all right now. Sorry to make you any trouble, sir."

He turned to push back the crowd, which was surging about the automobile now, and Mr. Horton lifted in Oliver. Then slowly, so as not to injure any one, he steered the car out of the mass of people and turned it around.

"Guess you'll stay in the car the next time, Oliver," jeered Harold Wallace.

"That'll do, Harold," said Mr. Horton sharply. "I'm going to take you all around the park twice now and then we'll scoot home for lunch. It is twelve o'clock. I don't want to take home such solemn faces. See if you can't smile a bit."

By the time they had circled the park twice every one felt decidedly more chee Even Oliver had managed a smile, though it would be some time before he could see a policeman and not want to run.

Sunny Boy had so much to tell Mother at lunch that he almost forgot to inform her of the loss of his hat. Seeing her trying on a new hat before the hall mirror after lunch reminded him.

"And how can I go to New York without a hat?" he finished sadly, when he had described to her how the colored boy had run off with his beautiful new, round, blue hat.

"You can't, of course," said Mother. "I'll have to take you down town again to-morrow and buy you another. Harriet, here's Sunny Boy losing his new hat before he's had it three days."

"Dear, dear! Do tell!" said Harriet, who was passing through the hall on her way upstairs. She sat down to listen.

"I might take Sunny down through the River Section," she suggested to Mrs. Horton. "We could go this afternoon. All the colored folks live there, you know, and Sunny might see the boy. I'd make him give the hat back, drat him!"

Mrs. Horton had little faith in their finding boy or hat, but she was willing they should go, and so Harriet and Sunny Boy set out half an hour later, bound for the River Section, which was over on the other side of the city from where the Hortons lived.

They decided to walk there and then ride home if they were tired, and Sunny Boy found much to interest him along the way. They passed a horse that had lost his nosebag before he had eaten all his oats and who was regarding it hungrily as it lay on the ground at his feet.

"Fix it, Harriet," implored Sunny. "He hasn't had all his dinner."

So Harriet stopped and picked up the nosebag and fixed it nicely on the horse's nose. He went right to eating the moment she had it in place, but Sunny Boy was sure his wise brown eyes thanked them gratefully.

"Look, Harriet!" they were crossing another street when Sunny Boy's quick eyes spied something else that interested him. "See, little desks."

A man was carrying desks into a brown stone house, and a large number of similar desks were propped up on the walk.

"'Miss May Ford's School for Boys and Girls.'" Harriet read the shining brass plate on the side of the house as they walked slowly past. "Why, Sunny, that must be the Miss May your mother talks about. I guess that's where you'll be going to school this winter."

Sunny Boy stared at the building with interest. He was very eager to learn what school was like, and he hoped that as soon as they came back from New York he would go to school every day as Nelson Baker did.

Two or three blocks further on Harriet turned suddenly down a side street.

"Now begin to look, Sunny," she admonished him. "See if you see a boy that looks like the one who took your hat this morning. How old would you say he was?"

"'Bout 'leven," returned Sunny Boy wisely. "He acted 'bout that, anyway. Isn't that a cunning baby, Harriet?"

Harriet wasn't interested in babies just then. She was determined to find that missing hat.

"That looks like him," Sunny pointed an accusing finger at a colored boy leaning against a rickety porch railing.

At the same moment the boy saw them and started to run.

"We can't chase him," said Harriet. "He'll run up some alley. You stay here on the sidewalk, and I'll ask if he lives in this house."

A little girl answered Harriet's knock. "Yes'm," she said, she knew the boy.

"He don't live here—don't live nowhere," she volunteered. "He just hangs around. His name is Pete."

"Well, there's no use in looking any further," announced Harriet, rejoining Sunny Boy on the pavement. "Pete, if that's his name, won't show up around here for several days now. And before that you'll be on your way to New York."

CHAPTER III
OFF FOR NEW YORK

"**S**unny Boy and I will go ahead and get the trunk checked," said Mr. Horton, picking up the two suitcases that stood in the hall. "Where's your hat? You haven't lost it again, have you?"

Sunny Boy dashed under the table and picked up his new hat.

"It's all right," he assured his father anxiously. "It just fell off when I wasn't looking. Mother bought it yesterday. Does it do for New York, Daddy?"

"I don't see why not," replied Mr. Horton, smiling. "All through, Olive? Sure you and Harriet can lock up all right?"

Mrs. Horton came into the hall, pencil and pad in hand. It was the day for leaving—Sunny Boy had been afraid that it would never come—and they were almost on the way to New York. The train would leave Centronia Union Station in an hour.

"I'm finishing the list of things I want Harriet to remember," explained Mrs. Horton. "Sunny, dear, did you say good-bye to her? All right then, run along with Daddy. And I'll meet you at the south entrance not later than a quarter of ten."

Sunny Boy and Daddy took the street car, and Sunny was so blissfully happy to be beginning the journey at last that a white-haired gentleman next to him asked him if he was thinking about Christmas.

Sunny Boy shook his head. He hadn't begun to think of Christmas. That was months and months away.

"I'm going to New York," he informed the white-haired gentleman proudly. "Daddy and Mother and me. And I can ride on top of the busses, Daddy said so."

"Dear me," said the gentleman, "that is a long trip for a chap of your age. I have a little grandson who lives in New York. He's counting the days now till he can come to see me."

This was a new idea to Sunny Boy.

"Do you s'pose folks who live in New York like to come to see Centronia?" he asked doubtfully.

"Just as much as you count on going to New York," said the white-haired gentleman promptly. "It's new to them, you see. Here's my corner now. Good-bye. I hope you will have all the good times you are looking forward to."

"Isn't it funny, Daddy?" said Sunny Boy, watching the gentleman go out the door. "Most everybody has relations living in New York. Harold Wallace's cousin lives there. Have we any 'lations to go to see?"

"Not in New York," answered Mr. Horton, pressing the button to tell the motor-man to let them off. "You and Mother will have to amuse each other, because you may find it lonesome at first with no friends to talk to."

They were opposite the station now, and the car stopped. Sunny Boy hopped off blithely, but his thoughts were busy with what Daddy had said. How could one be lonely in New York?

"'Member the time the baggage man thought the alarm clock was a 'fernal machine?" asked Sunny Boy, as he followed his father into the station and over to the baggage room.

"Indeed I do," Mr. Horton laughed.

You see, when Sunny Boy and his mother had been going to see Grandpa Horton, Sunny, as his part in the packing, tucked in the family alarm clock so that he would be sure to get up early in the country. And he forgot the clock might be set, as it was. The station people had held the trunk and it took a great deal of explaining, and the Hortons nearly missed their train before they were allowed to check the trunk.

The baggage man remembered Sunny Boy.

"How's the alarm clock?" he grinned cheerfully. "Any more infernal machines in your baggage this time?"

Sunny Boy smiled shyly.

"We didn't have a finger in packing this trunk," Daddy answered for him. "All right, Son, we're fixed. Now we'll see if we can get some parlor car seats."

But, it seemed, the parlor car seats were all sold.

"All the way through. Convention going to-day on your train," announced the man behind the brass-barred window. "Sorry, but you'll have to go in the day coach."

"You and I don't mind, Sunny," said Mr. Horton, as they walked over to the south entrance to wait for Mrs. Horton. "It is rather hard on Mother, but perhaps she won't mind. It isn't so warm to-day."

"And we can put the window up," suggested Sunny Boy helpfully. "Oh, there's Mother!"

He ran to meet her and brought her over triumphantly to the seat saved for her.

"Am I in time?" she asked a little anxiously. "Ten minutes yet? That's fine. There was a block on the cars."

"Get your breath, and then I think we'd better go through the gate," counseled Mr. Horton. "Couldn't get parlor car seats, so the earlier we get on, the better chance we have of getting a good seat. I'll take the grips, Sunny, you take care of Mother."

Sunny Boy felt that he was an experienced traveler when he handed the tickets to the man at the gate, Daddy's hands being occupied with the suitcases. The long gray train shed was filled with shining dark cars and snorting, puffing engines, but Daddy seemed to know where to go, and he led the way.

"This is all right," he decided, coming to a stop before a coach.

He put down the heavy suitcases and took the tickets from Sunny.

"They'll be safer in my wallet," he explained. "But you may give them to the conductor if you wish. Up you go—there!"

Sunny Boy found himself on the platform beside Mother, who had gone first. He followed her into the nearly dark car, and they found two nice seats near the center and on what Daddy said would be the shady side as soon as they pulled out of the shed.

"If a crowd comes in we must give up one of these seats," Mr. Horton said, turning back one so that it faced the other. "But until then let's be as comfortable as we can."

He put the suitcases in the racks overhead, put Mother's light dust coat up with them, and raised both windows. Sunny Boy and his mother sat facing Daddy.

"Now we're off," announced Mr. Horton, smiling at Sunny Boy, who was watching everything.

A few more people came into the car, but not many, and after what seemed a long wait to Sunny, they heard the conductor's long-drawn-out "All a-bo-ard!"

The train groaned and started slowly.

"And now we're going!" declared Sunny Boy, with satisfaction.

"Now we're going," echoed Mother. "Don't put your head out, Sunny. If the wind blows too strongly we'll have to put the window down."

Sunny Boy hoped it wouldn't blow too much. He loved to feel it rumpling his hair and cutting gently across his cheek.

"There's Haver's grocery," he cried, as they passed the red-brick store on a street corner. "And the market! There's where we punctured a tire, Daddy. And, look! There's where Harriet took her shoes to be mended!"

"Not so loud," cautioned Mr. Horton. Indeed, Sunny had unconsciously raised his voice, and several people were smiling at him.

So Sunny Boy made up a little song to amuse himself as the train went slowly through the city streets, streets he knew fairly well because he had ridden through them with his father in the automobile.

"Bicycle shop, gasoline station, fresh egg store," sang Sunny softly. "Mr. French's ice-cream—wonder if he'll know I've gone to New York."

Soon the train began to go faster, and Sunny Boy did not know the little towns they were passing through. Almost before he knew it, the waiter came through announcing lunch, and the Hortons went into the dining-car. This was the third time Sunny Boy had eaten on the train, and he was, as he said, "'Most used to it."

When they came back into their own coach, and had settled down, Mr. Horton to read his paper and Mrs. Horton with a book to read aloud to Sunny, a tall, thin, rather odd looking man who had sat huddled up in a corner seat suddenly clapped his hand to his eye and began to act strangely.

"Ow!" he cried. "Ow! I told you not to have that window opened. Oh! Oh, my! What shall I do?"

"He must be in a fit," said the woman in the seat behind the Hortons.

"Appendicitis, probably," declared the man across the aisle.

"Nonsense," said Mr. Horton briskly. "He has a cinder in his eye. I wonder if he would let me take it out for him?"

There was a crowd about the man now, and as Mr. Horton went down the aisle to help him, Sunny Boy slipped out of his seat, too, and tagged along after.

"I know something about first-aid," he heard his father say. "Let me look at your eye. Stand back, neighbors, we need a little room."

Watching, Sunny Boy managed to see his father take out a clean white handkerchief and a lead pencil. He seemed only to look at the man's eye, and then the cinder was out and the excitement over.

"If that boy hadn't opened his window, this never would have happened," declared the man, who was grateful to Mr. Horton for relieving his pain, but determined to lay his misfortune to some one. "I'm going into the smoker. Perhaps a man can have a little less fresh air and a bit more common sense in there."

He tramped angrily away. Sunny Boy looked for the first time at the boy in the seat ahead, who had been leaning over the back apologetically, fearful that his open window really had caused the trouble.

"Why, Joe Brown!" said Sunny Boy.

Joe turned a dull red. He was a boy whom Sunny did not know very well, and he was a number of years older, twelve or thirteen years old at least. His mother often did sewing for Mrs. Horton, and Sunny sometimes saw Joe at Sunday school and at the grocery store where he sometimes worked after school.

"Hullo, Sunny," said Joe Brown awkwardly. "Where you goin'?"

"To New York," announced Sunny Boy importantly. "Where you going?"

"To New York," was the answer.

"How do you do, Joe?" asked Mr. Horton kindly, coming up to him. "Taking a trip, too, are you?"

"Yes, sir," mumbled Joe. "Going to see my Aunt Annabell in New York."

"Where does she live?" said Mr. Horton with interest. "Perhaps we can drop you there on our way from the station. Do you plan to stay long?"

Joe Brown fumbled with his cap.

"I don't know just how long I'll stay," he blurted out. "Maybe all winter. I've got Auntie's address somewhere in my satchel. I know how to get there all right."

Mr. Horton went back to his seat, but Sunny Boy lingered.

"You're another with 'lations in New York," he observed. "Harold Wallace has a cousin, and the gentleman on the street car had a grandson. I wish my Aunt Bessie lived in New York. Have you been there before?"

"No, I haven't," admitted Joe Brown. "But I guess one city's pretty much like another. I went to Chicago when I was six. I'm going to see all the big places when I'm grown up."

"There's Mother motioning to me," said Sunny Boy. "Come on and see her."

But Joe Brown wouldn't.

"I have to write a letter," he protested hastily.

Sunny Boy went back to his parents. He had an odd feeling that Joe Brown was not looking forward to seeing New York as much as he, Sunny Boy, was.

"Is he sick, do you think, Daddy?" he urged, his troubled eyes resting on Joe, now huddled moodily in his seat and making no pretense of letter-writing.

"No, he's all right," said Mr. Horton easily. "Come, laddie, we're almost at the end of our trip. Sit down by Mother and see your first glimpse of one of the largest cities in the world."

Sunny Boy scrambled into his place again, but Joe Brown was still in his thoughts. Presently he heard his father speaking in a low voice to his mother.

"Olive, I believe that young scamp, the Brown boy, is running away from home. He has it written all over him. I wish we could keep an eye on him."

20

"But Mrs. Brown has a sister who lives in New York," said Sunny Boy's mother. "He may really be going to visit her."

"Perhaps," admitted Mr. Horton doubtfully.

There was no time to say more just then for the train rushed down from daylight into what was next to darkness.

"Oh!" cried Sunny Boy, "where are we going, Mother? Are we in a cellar?"

"We are going down under the Hudson River into New York," explained Mrs. Horton. "That will save us the trouble of going over on a ferryboat."

Sunny Boy was very much interested in the ride under the river and asked many questions.

"I should think the river would leak in on us," he remarked. "And we haven't any umbrellas along."

"We are perfectly safe," his father assured him.

Then in a few minutes the bustle of getting ready to leave the train began.

"We'll take a taxi," announced Mr. Horton, holding his wife's coat for her. "Take Mother's hand, Sunny. Careful, now."

Down the steps on to the platform, where Mr. Horton gave the suitcases to a porter, and they joined a steady stream of people all going in one direction.

CHAPTER IV
GOING SHOPPING

"**O**h, look! There's a bus! Let's ride on top," cried Sunny Boy, pointing out toward the street as one of the Fifth Avenue busses lumbered into sight.

"But our taxi is here," reasoned Mr. Horton, helping in Sunny Boy's mother as he spoke. "And I couldn't go up on top with these heavy bags. Come, Son, and you shall have your ride to-morrow."

Sunny Boy climbed into the taxi cab, Mr. Horton followed, and they were on the way to their hotel.

It was a brief ride, but in those few moments Sunny Boy was sure he had seen more automobiles than he had ever seen in his life. He probably had, for it was the time of day when the city traffic is heaviest, and never-ending streams of motor-cars and trucks and wagons were being driven on the cross streets, as well as on the avenues.

"I feel as if I wasn't here," said Sunny Boy slowly, watching the crowds from the open window.

Mr. Horton glanced down at him and smiled.

"You do look rather small in all this," he admitted; "but I should say you were very much here. And here's our hotel, and I think you are ready for supper."

The taxi cab stopped before the McAlpin Hotel, and Sunny Boy, holding fast to Daddy's hand, went into a beautiful high-ceilinged room ablaze with light. He and his mother sat down in one of the big chairs while Mr. Horton registered and arranged for their room. Then a severe-faced boy took the suitcases and led them into an elevator.

"I wonder if he's cross," thought Sunny Boy to himself, studying the face of the boy as he stood stiffly, his eyes fixed grimly on the wire grating of the elevator.

He was staring at him so hard that when the boy turned and caught him Sunny Boy blushed. The boy stuck out his tongue and immediately resumed his stern expression.

"He wears such a lot of buttons," thought Sunny Boy, who in all his life had never been in a hotel to stay over night. "I wonder did he really stick out his tongue—"

The elevator stopped while Sunny Boy was trying to decide, and the Hortons followed the boy along a silent corridor till he stopped before a door and, unlocking it, ushered them into a large, pleasant room.

"Well, dear, hungry?" asked Mrs. Horton.

"He did it again," said Sunny Boy.

"Who did what?" laughed Mrs. Horton. "Sunny, don't let New York addle you like this. I asked if you were hungry."

"That boy did stick out his tongue," explained Sunny Boy. "I don't guess he is cross at all. When he closed the door he winked at me. And I am hungry, Mother."

Supper, as Sunny Boy insisted on calling it, or dinner, was rather a vague affair to him, for he was not only hungry but very sleepy after the long train ride. He liked riding down in the elevator and up again, but he was glad enough to go to bed.

"It's just like the three bears," he said to Mother as she helped him to undress. "Big Bear, Middle-sized Bear, and Little Bear," he added, pointing to the three beds in the room. "Did they know I was coming and put a little bed in for me?"

"Daddy asked them to," said Mother. "Now a little wash, precious, and you'll be in Dreamland in two seconds."

There was a pretty white bathroom opening into the room, and Sunny Boy enjoyed a splash, and then tumbled into bed.

In the morning he had a hard time to get dressed, because he found it so interesting to stare out of the window down at the busy streets.

"Such lots of people and trolley cars and automobiles—and everything!" he reported to his mother, who insisted that he really must finish dressing. "Do you suppose they know I'm looking at 'em?"

"I doubt it," said Mother, brushing his hair smooth. "Now don't put your nose on the screen again, Sunny. We're going downstairs in just a minute. Daddy is almost through shaving."

"You look dressed up, Mother," announced Sunny Boy critically. "And aren't we going to eat breakfast first?"

"First?" repeated Mrs. Horton, puzzled. "Oh, you mean I have my hat and veil on. Well, dear, I believe you and I are going out right after breakfast, and I won't have to come upstairs again. Ready, Daddy?"

Soon they were in the dining room.

"Where are we going?" asked Sunny Boy, at the table and trying not to feel queer when the waiter brought him his cantaloupe with the same flourish with which he served Daddy sitting opposite.

"Why, I'm going to be very busy this morning," explained Mr. Horton, "and I thought you and Mother might enjoy a little shopping trip. I'll meet you here for lunch. Anything you specially want to buy, Sunny?"

"Some post cards," replied Sunny Boy promptly. "Ruth Nelson wants one for her collection. And I could get Aunt Bessie a present."

"I'd wait till we're almost ready to go home for Aunt Bessie's present," said Mr. Horton kindly. "You'll know better what you want then. But get the post cards by all means this morning."

He gave Sunny Boy a bright new fifty-cent piece.

"I think we'll walk," decided Mrs. Horton, serving the golden brown omelet carefully. "Put your money in your new purse, dear. Harry, have you heard from Mr. Vernon yet?"

Left to himself while his parents talked business matters, Sunny Boy looked about the dining room. He saw several children, little girls and boys here and there, and a little girl across the room nodded and smiled at him. Sunny Boy wondered where the boy who had carried up their suitcases was.

"I didn't bring my hat," he mourned when breakfast was over. "Can I go and get it, Mother?"

"I brought it down, dear," was the answer. "We're going right away. Daddy has some telephoning to do, and we'll go on."

In the hotel lobby Sunny Boy saw the suitcase boy, as he had named him, again. He didn't seem quite so severe as he had at night, and when Sunny smiled at him he actually returned it with a grin that showed a set of very white teeth.

"What a funny carriage," said Sunny Boy, calling Mother's attention to a queer looking vehicle on two wheels and drawn by a bob-tailed horse, which was the first thing he saw when they got out on the street. "Look where the coachman is."

The driver was perched up on a little seat behind and held the reins over the roof of the coach.

"That's a hansom cab," explained Mrs. Horton. "They were very popular and stylish before the automobile came."

Privately Sunny Boy thought it wasn't very handsome, and the poor old horse was no longer stylish if he had ever been, but there was little time to think about hansom cabs, for just then Mother remarked:

"Here's the big store where they have such a wonderful toy department."

It was a big store, much larger than any Sunny Boy had ever seen in Centronia, and it seemed filled with people to him.

"Oh, Mother!" he stopped so short that several people nearly fell over him, "what's that?"

"That" was a long shining moving thing on which people were being wafted gently upward. It reminded Sunny Boy of the fairy tale he had seen in the motion picture where the Wishing Girl who wanted to fly was suddenly granted her wish.

"Where do they go?" Sunny Boy asked so loudly that a floor-man heard and answered him.

"That's an escalator," he announced, much as one might say: "That's a strawberry."

"It's a moving stairway, precious," added his mother. "I suppose you want to ride on it. Well, first I must get Daddy some handkerchiefs, for we never packed him a one. And we'll find out on which floor the toys are, too."

Sunny Boy waited patiently while the handkerchiefs were bought, and then while Mother chose a new veil, a pretty white one with black dots.

"Here are the post-cards, Sunny," she said, turning into another aisle. "See which ones you want for Ruth and Nelson."

"What do they say, Mother?" asked Sunny Boy, wishing he could read. "May I send all the boys some?"

Mrs. Horton said he could, and she helped him select a dozen views of New York, promising that he should print his name on each one and that she would write whatever messages he wanted sent.

"You can look them over this afternoon," she suggested, "and see what places you want to see first. That will be nice, won't it?"

"Yes, Mother," agreed Sunny Boy. "And now can we ride on the alligator?"

"The escalator?" corrected Mother, laughing heartily. "Why yes, I think we are about ready to do that. The girl at the handkerchief counter told me the toys were on the sixth floor. Do you think you want to ride that far on such a queer thing?"

"He had not supposed that a moving stairs went further than one story"

Sunny Boy was enraptured. He had not supposed that a moving stairway went further than one story, and the thought of riding to the sixth floor was bliss. He felt decidedly odd when he put his foot on the moving platform at first, but ahead of him and behind him people were serenely moving up, so he knew everything must be all right. When he reached the top he slid off with such an unexpected bump that he gave a startled cry and the girl who was there to see that no one was hurt laughed at him.

"You said we could go to the sixth floor!" exclaimed Sunny Boy, turning aggrievedly to Mother who had followed him.

"And so we can, dear, but not without stopping," explained Mrs. Horton. "See, we turn here and there is another escalator. At every floor we get off one and then on another."

Sunny Boy thought this was absolutely the most delightful way of going upstairs he had ever tried. He wondered why the stores at home didn't have moving stairways, and he resolved to come down the whole six flights the same way. He was astonished when the time came to go home and he found that the escalators didn't carry people down, but only up.

"I see a horse!" he shouted, when they were half way up the last stairway.

They stepped off onto a floorful of toys that reminded Sunny Boy of Christmas and birthdays and Santa Claus all rolled into one. A tank of water in which boats were sailing caught his eye.

"I wish I'd brought my boat," he remarked, standing on tiptoe to see over the edge. "See the motor-boat, Mother? It's just like Captain Franklin's."

Captain Franklin was the man who had found Sunny Boy when he was drifting out to sea in a rowboat that summer, as related in the book called "Sunny Boy at the Seashore."

"If you want to see them race," said the young man in charge of the boats, "I'll wind another up for you."

CHAPTER V
SUNNY BOY LOSES HIS ROOM

O f course Sunny Boy wanted to see the boats race, and he hung breathlessly over the edge of the tank while the good-natured clerk wound up the motor-boats and sent them racing across several times.

"Come, dear," Mrs. Horton urged at last. "You haven't seen the trains yet, nor the rocking-horses. And Daddy will be waiting for us at one, you know."

So Sunny Boy, very reluctantly, thanked the man in charge of the boats and walked down the aisle to see the mechanical trains.

Goodness! the trains were more fascinating than the boats. There were miles and miles of track, and little colored signal lights, and stations and tunnels and freight and coal and passenger trains, with freight and coal and passengers to go in them.

"All running!" marveled Sunny Boy. "Just like Christmas!"

Mrs. Horton was trying to pull him past this absorbing counter, for they really had a great deal more to see and the time was getting short, when Sunny gave a shout.

"Mother, look! There's a runaway engine! Whee, a wreck!"

Sure enough, an engine with no cars attached was coming rapidly down grade toward a passenger train stopped at one of the stations. Sunny Boy's voice had drawn a number of the shoppers, and a small crowd gathered to see what would happen. The clerk had left the counter and gone out to an aisle table to have a floor-man sign his book, and there was no one about to prevent the wreck.

Smash! with a truly thrilling noise the engine crashed into the train and the passengers must have, as the newspapers say, "received a severe shaking up."

"Oh, gee!" breathed Sunny Boy, and his sigh was echoed by the grown-ups.

People looked at one another and smiled.

"Nobody hurt!" announced the clerk, who had hurried back when he heard the noise of the collision. "I said that switch needed overhauling yesterday. Guess I'll shut off the current and get a repair man to come up."

As there would be no more moving trains for the present, Sunny Boy was willing to go to see the rocking-horses. He had a fine time, too, for the clerk lifted him up on the largest one, and very high from the ground Sunny felt.

But it was the tin automobile that captured his heart.

"Oh, Mother!" he said when he found it, "it's just like our car, two lamps and all."

"It is pretty nice," admitted Mrs. Horton. "We'll have to see what Daddy says about one when we go home. You are getting too old for the kiddie car, aren't you? How does this one run, dear?"

Sunny Boy showed her, and explained how the brakes worked, and they had an interesting half-hour comparing the different kinds of cars and learning how much they cost. Then Mother discovered that it was time to go back to the hotel if they were to meet Daddy promptly.

"I could stay here," suggested Sunny Boy, his arm about a stuffed camel that was almost large enough for him to ride. His jaw went up and down if you poked it right, and he had two most realistic humps. "You could go and see Daddy and then come back and get me."

"But, precious, what would Daddy say? He'll want to see you. And there will be many other times for you to come over and visit the toys. Besides, think, Sunny—suppose he wanted to take you riding on the Fifth Avenue bus?"

That settled it. Sunny Boy was ready to go immediately. Anyway, he realized that he had a queer feeling he couldn't just name, but he suspected that maybe he was hungry.

They found Mr. Horton waiting for them in their room, and Mrs. Horton had so much to tell him that Sunny Boy had to wait his chance to ask a most important question.

"Daddy," he began when his father finished telling the waiter what to bring, and after they were in the dining room and seated at the table, "Daddy, do you think p'haps we could go riding on the bus?"

Mr. Horton smiled.

"Well, I'll tell you," he said, glancing at his watch. "Mother wants to lie down and rest a bit this afternoon and I have to meet some men within an hour. But if you are a good boy, I'll take you when I come back. That will be about three o'clock. How'll that do?"

Sunny Boy thought that would be very nice, and he ate his luncheon contentedly. Afterward he and Mother went upstairs, and Daddy had to go and keep his appointment.

"Now you see how much company we are for each other," said Mother, as she changed her dress and put on a pretty blue dressing gown. "With such a busy Daddy, wouldn't we be lonesome here in New York all alone?"

Sunny Boy nodded solemnly.

"Could I paint pictures?" he asked hopefully.

"Of course. You'll find your paint box and a pad of paper in that grey box in the trunk tray. Mother's going to lie down just a second. Pull the little table over to the light, dear, and you'll have a nice, quiet time," directed Mrs. Horton.

Sunny Boy dragged the table over nearer to the window, found his water color paints and the paper and set to work to paint a picture. He talked a steady stream to Mother at first but, as he grew interested in his work, he forgot to talk.

"There now!" he said softly, when he had finished three pictures. "I think they're good. I'll show 'em to Mother."

But Mother was fast asleep. Sunny Boy tiptoed carefully around the bed, but she did not wake up.

"I don't want to paint any more," decided Sunny Boy. "What'll I do?"

He remembered the bell-boy they had seen first the night before. He would go and visit him.

Sunny Boy opened the door into the corridor carefully, so as not to disturb Mother, and closed it carefully behind him. The halls were lighted, though it was daytime, and the thick carpet was so soft that Sunny couldn't hear the noise of his own feet.

"Where 'bouts," he speculated aloud, "do they have the stairs in this house?"

He hunted for several minutes, but no stairs could he find. Then he decided to go back to Mother, and he couldn't find the room! He had made so many turnings in the halls that he was hopelessly lost.

"Oh, dear!" sighed poor Sunny Boy. "New York is such a big place!"

A light down the corridor attracted his attention now. The elevator, of course! Why hadn't he thought of that? He would find the bell-boy downstairs. He remembered that was where he had seen him at breakfast time.

The elevator boy took him downstairs without asking any questions and let him off at the first floor.

"This looks somehow different," puzzled Sunny Boy, standing where the elevator left him.

He didn't know it, but it was another elevator, in a different part of the building from the one his father and mother took down to the dining room. Sunny Boy had never been downstairs alone, and he felt decidedly shy.

"Hello, kid, what you lost?" asked one of the bell boys, swinging past him.

"Nothing," murmured Sunny Boy.

"Are you lost, dear?" asked a lady, stopping on her way to the elevator. She was old and lame and walked with a cane. A maid, with a curly black dog under her arm, walked beside her.

Sunny shook his head. How could he be lost with a mother in the same building with him? Of course he wasn't lost!

He sat down in a leather chair to consider. He didn't know the name of the bell boy he wanted to see, and at any minute his father might come back and want to take him for a ride on the bus. Sunny Boy made up his mind that he would try to find his room and look for the bell boy another time. He waited till a friendly-looking man came hurrying by where he sat.

"Please," he stuttered nervously, "how do you find—"

"Ask the clerk at the desk!" snapped the man, who wasn't cross, but only in a hurry to make a train.

Sunny Boy looked about for the desk.

"Go 'round there," directed the elevator boy when he ventured to ask him. Then he clashed his door shut with a bang and went sailing up in his little car.

Sunny obediently wandered around a turn in the corridor. He saw only a counter, but he guessed that to be the desk. He remembered it was where his father had gone to arrange for their rooms the night before.

"Please," he began, standing on tiptoes and grasping the edge of the counter with both hands. "Please, where is our room?"

"Eh, what?" demanded the startled clerk, bending down to see the small person speaking to him. "Your room? Have you lost your key?"

"Haven't any key," explained Sunny Boy gravely. "I came out, and when I went to go back I couldn't find our door."

"All right, we'll fix you up," promised the clerk. "Jack, lift this young man up so I won't have to strain my voice."

A bell-boy lifted Sunny to the counter, and he sat there comfortably, sure that the clerk would solve his troubles for him.

"What floor are you on?" asked the clerk capably.

"I don't know," confessed Sunny Boy.

"Well, then, give us your name."

"Sunny Boy," announced Sunny cheerfully.

The clerk laughed, and the bell-boys standing about snickered.

"No Sunny Boy registered," announced the clerk, running his finger down the register, where hotel guests write their names. "Haven't you any other name you use when you're traveling around?"

"Oh, no," insisted Sunny Boy. "Daddy and Mother always call me that—just Sunny Boy."

"But you have to have a regular name," protested the clerk. "When you go to school—Oh, you don't go to school! Well, what is Daddy's name? Your last name must be the same as his."

Then Sunny Boy understood.

"Daddy's name is Harry Horton, and I am named for Grandpa, Arthur Bradford Horton," he announced rapidly. "An' we live in Centronia."

"Now you're talking," said the clerk approvingly. "Here you are." He read from the big register: "'Mr. and Mrs. Harry Horton and son'. You're son. And your room is 1038. Jack, you take him up, will you? Is any one there, or have they gone out and left you alone?"

Sunny Boy explained that his mother was lying down, and Jack lifted him from the counter and went over with him to the elevator.

"He lost his room," he told the elevator boy as they shot up. "Didn't you bring him down?"

"Must have come down in one of the other cars," said the elevator boy. "I don't remember him. Here's your floor."

Jack showed Sunny Boy which was the door to his room, and, still grinning at the idea of losing one's way in a hotel, he went back.

"Why, Sunny dear, where have you been?" Mrs. Horton was sitting up in bed as Sunny Boy came in. "I woke up a minute ago and thought you were still painting. Then I spoke to you and found you weren't in the room. Where did you go?"

"I got lost," said Sunny Boy placidly.

He told his mother what had happened and she laughed.

"Here's Daddy," she announced, as some one rapped on the door. "Come in, Harry. Sunny Boy's adventures in New York have already begun."

So Mr. Horton heard the story.

"Well, well, we'll have to go out for our ride, or there's no knowing what will happen next," he said jokingly. "Want to come, Olive?"

Mrs. Horton answered that she didn't want to dress hurriedly and that she would rather wait for them and write a letter or two, perhaps.

"I'll help you write your post cards in the morning," she promised Sunny Boy. "Harriet will be expecting a card from you every day till it comes."

Sunny Boy and his father went out of the hotel and walked over toward Fifth Avenue. The trolley cars and automobiles and crowds of people seemed to Sunny Boy to be hopelessly mixed. He held tightly to Daddy's hand when they crossed the street, and he was very grateful to the tall policeman that made the traffic stop while the people surged safely across.

"Up top, you know, Daddy," he urged, trotting along, trying to keep step with his father's long stride.

"All right, up top we'll go," said Mr. Horton, smiling. "I thought we'd walk around to the Pennsylvania station and get a bus there. We may want to go home from there instead of the way we came."

CHAPTER VI
ON TOP OF THE BUS

The Pennsylvania Station is a beautiful building, but Sunny Boy hardly saw it, so eager was he to climb up the winding stairs on one of the busses.

"Are we going up, or down?" he chattered to Daddy, as they stood on the curb.

"Over first," explained Mr. Horton, "and then up. I thought we might go as far as Grant's Tomb; then you can see the river, and to-morrow, if Mother likes to, we will go down and through the Arch at Washington Square."

A bus came up and stopped presently, and Sunny Boy was afraid there would be no room left for him, so many people seemed to want to ride outside and enjoy the fine September afternoon.

"Careful, now," cautioned Mr. Horton, as he guided Sunny Boy up the narrow, steep stairs. "They will start before you get to the top."

Sure enough, the bus did start, but Sunny Boy had a firm grip on the iron railing. He thought it great fun to be going upstairs on a moving automobile, and when he reached the top, the very first seat, away up front, was vacant!

"P'haps I'd better take my hat off," he suggested, as he snuggled into the seat next the railing and Daddy sat down beside him. "The colored boy took my first one, you know, and if I lost this one Mother might not like it."

"Indeed she might not," agreed Mr. Horton. "Neither should I, because new hats cost money. You'll be more comfortable holding it, anyway."

Sunny Boy took it off then, and held it in his lap. When the conductor came for their fares, he held out a funny-looking thing and said they were to put the money in that.

"Let me," begged Sunny Boy.

Daddy gave him two ten-cent pieces, and he put them in the little slit and heard the bell ring twice.

Sunny Boy had never been so happy. He liked to look down from the high top of the bus and watch the motors and the people in the street. At nearly every cross street they had to stop while traffic went the other way, and often there would be four or five automobiles abreast. Once Sunny, looking down, saw a little boy in a beautiful car looking up at him. Sunny Boy waved, and the little boy smiled delightedly and waved back. Then the whistle blew and the car shot far ahead of the slow-running bus.

"Where are we going now?" demanded Sunny, as their bus turned.

"Wait and see," smiled Mr. Horton.

And in a minute Sunny Boy saw on one side of him a row of handsome houses, on the other a strip of cement walk and a green park, and beyond that water that sparkled in the sun.

"This is Riverside Drive," said Mr. Horton. "See, Son, those are battleships anchored out there."

Sunny Boy stood up to see better, while Daddy steadied him. He had never seen a battleship before except in pictures.

"What funny wire cages," he puzzled. "And see the little boat going out to them, Daddy."

"Those wire 'cages' as you call them, are masts," explained his father. "And the little boat is probably carrying some officers or sailors out to their ship. That is as near as the battleships can come to the land, you see."

Sunny Boy wanted to know why, and Mr. Horton told him that the water wasn't deep enough close in shore.

"If you want to see a battleship better, perhaps go aboard one, we must visit the Navy Yard before we go home," he remarked.

Sunny Boy was sure he would like that.

The battleships were left far behind now, and a man and woman riding horseback attracted Sunny's attention. He thought it must be fun to have a horse and go riding along such a beautiful drive.

"I could roller skate and Harriet could knit like that," he suggested, pointing to a boy skating merrily up and down while a white-capped nurse sat on a bench and knitted comfortably.

"Yes, you could," said his father. "But since Harriet isn't here, you'll have to write her about what you've seen instead. We get off at the next corner, Sunny; press the little black button there by your hand."

Sunny Boy pressed the button which rang the bell to tell the bus driver to stop, and he and Mr. Horton walked to the stairs. Sunny was very glad to have his father go first, because he discovered that coming downstairs was more ticklish than going up. He had a feeling that he was going to pitch forward on his yellow head.

However, they both reached the ground safely, and, his hand in Daddy's, Sunny Boy crossed over and stood at the flight of broad steps that led to Grant's Tomb.

"Do you know who General Grant was, dear?" asked Daddy.

Sunny Boy nodded his head.

"Grandpa told me," he said confidently. "He was in the Civil War."

"Yes, he was a general in the Civil War, and later president of the United States," assented Mr. Horton. "And this beautiful building was given by the people who loved and admired him, as a memorial."

They went up the wide steps and entered the rotunda. The light was subdued, and at first Sunny Boy could see nothing. Then he saw several people, the men with their hats in their hands, looking down what he thought was a deep well.

Daddy lifted him up so that he might look over, and there, down on the marble floor, he saw two American flags draped over two oblong stone slabs and a wreath on each.

"Mrs. Grant is buried here, too," said Mr. Horton.

The old, battle-stained flags and war mementos in the two little alcoves off the rotunda would have interested Sunny's Grandpa Horton, who had seen some of those same flags carried on the battle fields, but one couldn't expect Sunny Boy to care much about them. When they came out and stood once more on the steps in the sunshine, he saw something that interested him more.

"Daddy!" he raised his voice in excitement. "What are those funny boats'? Over there—see? There's two of 'em!"

A young man standing near heard and turned with a grin.

"Where did you hail from, kid?" he asked curiously. "Haven't you ever seen a ferryboat before?"

Sunny Boy hated to be laughed at, so he said nothing.

"We're inland folks," explained Mr. Horton, who didn't seem to mind the young man's smile. "Out where we live no rivers connect our cities. My little boy has seen his first ferryboat to-day."

"I've seen *boats*," said Sunny Boy with dignity. "I saw them down at the seashore. But not like those. What do they use 'em for?"

The young man laughed again.

"Excuse me," he apologized. "But I've crossed the river every morning for ten years on the ferry, and it strikes me as funny to find some one who doesn't know what a ferryboat is. They carry people and horses and automobiles, kid."

"Horses?" repeated Sunny Boy incredulously. "Come on, Daddy, let's go ride on one."

"That's the Fort Lee Ferry. Nothing much to see," advised the young man, who was good-natured if he did laugh at folks. "Better go down town and take the Twenty-third Street, if you want a nice sail."

"Thank you, we will, when we do go," replied Mr. Horton. "But, Sunny, you and I must be getting back to Mother. She will be wondering what has become of us. See if you can signal a bus."

"Sunny Boy was just the least little bit afraid when they went under the elevator tracks"

Sunny Boy stopped a bus very nicely, and again they found a seat on the top. Sunny Boy was just the least little bit afraid when they went under the elevated tracks—they didn't have elevated trains in Centronia—and he hoped nothing would drop on him.

"What a lot of things there are to ride on in New York," he confided to Daddy. "Busses, an' trains up high, and ferryboats, and automobiles and trolley cars like at home."

"And another kind of train you don't know about yet," said Mr. Horton. "What is it? Oh, I'm going to let you find out for yourself. You seem to be developing a liking for riding about on all kinds of transportation."

"Well, I would like to go on a ferryboat," admitted Sunny Boy, "an' maybe on the elevated. An' the other kind of train that I don't know about. And that's all."

They found Mrs. Horton dressed for dinner and awaiting them, and while she helped Sunny to put on a clean suit and brush his hair, he told her about their trip and what they had seen on Riverside Drive.

"And Daddy says if you want to, we can ride on the bus to-morrow," he finished. "We can go and see an arch."

Mr. Horton, who had been reading some letters that had come for him while he and Sunny were out, looked up from the little book in which he wrote the things he wanted to remember.

"I'm sorry, but you and Mother will have to amuse each other to-morrow," he announced. "I shall be busy all day. But I think you can manage to have a pleasant time, and perhaps the next day I can go about with you."

"Of course we'll have a happy day," promised Mrs. Horton. "Don't worry about us, Daddy Horton. We know you are on a business trip. I think Sunny Boy and I will plan to spend the day in Central Park."

"Yes, let's," agreed Sunny Boy enthusiastically.

He had not the smallest idea what Central Park was like, but he was very sure that he would like it. He liked everything that he had seen in New York so far.

As the Hortons came out of the dining room, and Mr. Horton stopped to buy a paper, Sunny Boy saw the bell-boy he had tried to visit that afternoon.

"Hello," he remarked conversationally. "I was looking for you this afternoon."

"Were you the kid that got lost?" chuckled the bell-boy. "Jack said to me: 'Frank, there was a boy couldn't find his own room this afternoon, can you believe it?' And what have you been doing with yourself all day?"

Sunny Boy recounted his adventures, and announced that the next day he and Mother were going to Central Park.

"Be sure you go in the Monkey House," counseled Frank. "I tell you those monkeys are the cutest things you ever saw. Almost human, I'll say. Like monkeys?"

"Yes in pictures," said Sunny Boy. "And those the organ grinders have. Here comes Daddy."

Before he went to sleep that night Sunny Boy thought of something he wanted to ask Frank.

"I will the next time I see him," he muttered drowsily.

He was wondering why he never put his cap on straight, but always wore it a little over one ear.

CHAPTER VII
IN CENTRAL PARK

T he next morning Sunny Boy and Mother started early for Central Park. Much to Sunny's delight they took a bus, and though they did not have very far to go, Mother climbed up to the top with him. When they got off at the Park gate they found carriages waiting for those who wanted to drive around the park.

"I think we should like that, don't you?" asked Mrs. Horton. "I'm sure we can not hope to walk all over this great place in one day. Shall we drive, dear?"

"Let's," nodded Sunny Boy. "I like that fat, black horse, Mother."

So they got into the carriage pulled by the fat, black horse and driven by a young man so tall that he couldn't sit up straight in the seat or his head would have hit the roof of the carriage.

"Is Central Park bigger than Brookside?" Sunny Boy asked, as they drove over a well-kept road past the greenest of green lawns and bright flower beds. Brookside was the name of Grandpa Horton's farm.

"How big is Brookside?" asked the driver, slapping the reins to make his horse go faster.

"Oh, ever so big," Sunny Boy assured him. "Seventy-nine acres, Daddy said."

"Well, you could put Brookside right down in Central Park and never see it," announced the driver complacently. "This park has eight hundred and seventy-nine acres."

"Gee!" murmured Sunny Boy.

He was silent for a few moments, trying to imagine how large the park must be.

"What a funny way to hay," he remarked, as they came up to a horse tramping steadily over the grass pulling a machine that looked something like a mower. "Grandpa didn't do it that way."

"They're cutting the grass," explained the driver of the carriage. "Guess you haven't seen one of those machines. If they had only a lawn mower like the one your father uses on your lawn at home, you know, the grass would never get cut in one summer."

"Can't we get out?" Mrs. Horton asked next. "I'd like to go up and see the reservoirs."

"Sure you can," was the quick response. "I'll wait right here for you. Suppose you'll want to go in the snake house, too, and see the menagerie and the monkeys."

"Frank said to see the monkeys, didn't he, Mother?" said Sunny Boy. "But he didn't say anything about snakes."

They were out of the carriage now and walking toward the reservoirs.

"No, and I don't believe we want to see the snakes," returned Mrs. Horton. "I don't like them very much, and if you don't care I'd much rather see the monkeys. They can do so many funny tricks."

Sunny Boy didn't care about snakes, and he forgot them right away when he saw the gallons of water, spread out like a smooth lake.

"Is it all to drink?" he wanted to know. "Can't they go swimming in it, Mother? Where does it come from?"

"I'm afraid I don't know where the water comes from," admitted Mrs. Horton, "but we know it must be piped from miles and miles away. Think of all the thirsty people in New York who are glad to get a cool, clean drink this warm day."

"Wouldn't they like to swim in it?" insisted Sunny Boy.

"My, no, precious! No one must swim in water that is to be drunk, you must know that. Now we'll go back to our carriage, or the driver will be tired of waiting."

When they came to the menagerie and the monkey house, Mrs. Horton decided not to keep the carriage standing. She did not know how long they would be, and she knew that they could easily get back to the street and car lines again. She paid the driver and he drove off, whistling merrily.

"Let's see the bears, first," suggested Sunny Boy.

And they did. Sunny Boy pressed so close to the cages of the animals that his mother pulled him back repeatedly. They saw lions and tigers and bears and elephants and more queer and curious animals than Sunny Boy dreamed existed.

"I like the bears best," he told Mother, as they came away. "The polar bear looked just like our fur rug at home. And he had cakes of ice to sleep on."

"That is because he is used to cold weather," explained Mrs. Horton. "The polar bear isn't well or happy unless his den is nice and cold."

In the monkey house Sunny Boy was fascinated by one little black-faced monkey that kept running up to the top of his cage, swinging across, and then hanging by his tail at the other end before he dropped with a bang that would shake any one else's teeth loose.

"Doesn't he get a headache?" asked Sunny Boy aloud.

A boy who had been standing with his nose pressed against the cage bars, a rather shabby-looking boy with big holes in his tan stockings, answered without turning around.

"He's been doing that for the last hour," said the boy. "I think some one was mean to him early this morning and he is just mad."

Sunny moved closer to the other boy.

"You *are* Joe Brown, aren't you?" he asked, puzzled.

The boy turned sharply, and they saw that it was Joe Brown. A shabbier Joe Brown than he had been on the train, and with a pinched hungry look on his face that went to Mrs. Horton's heart.

"Did you find your aunt, Joe?" she asked kindly. "And do you like New York?"

Joe snatched off his cap awkwardly when Mrs. Horton spoke to him, and he tried to stuff it into his pocket now as he shuffled his feet and mumbled that he liked New York pretty well. Plainly he was not comfortable.

"Aunt Annabell moved away," he explained. "I went to the house, but Italians were living in it and they didn't know where she'd moved to. But I guess I can find her. Folks don't drop out of sight in New York."

"But where are you staying?" said Mrs. Horton. "What do you do? Can't I or Mr. Horton help you, Joe? A boy alone in a great city like this might need a friend, you know."

Joe Brown scuffled his feet uneasily.

"I'm all right," he insisted.

"Well, at least come and have some lunch with Sunny and me," invited Mrs. Horton. "Perhaps you can tell us some place to go? And then come up to the hotel with us this afternoon and we'll see if Mr. Horton can't find out something about your aunt."

Joe knew of a place where lunch could be had, and he and Mrs. Horton and Sunny Boy were soon seated at a white-topped little table eating sandwiches and milk. Joe ate as though he were half-starved, and Mrs. Horton pretended to be hungrier than she was so that he would not be afraid to eat all the sandwiches he wanted.

"Has Sunny seen the carrousel?" Joe demanded, when the ice-cream had been brought and Sunny was deep in the blissful employment of scooping spoonfuls out of the white mound before him.

"No, I haven't," answered Sunny quickly.

"Well you'll like it—it's like a big playground," explained Joe. "Swings, merry-go-rounds, all that kind of stuff, you know. And it's pretty around there, too. I'll take you if you want to see it."

After they had finished lunch he did take them, and he was very good and patient, too, about swinging Sunny Boy and giving him rides on all the contrivances that make small people happy.

"Let the old cat die," called Sunny Boy, as he was being swung for the third time.

Slower and slower went the swing, and finally it stopped. Sunny Boy sat still, expecting Joe to come and lift him out, but no Joe came. Mrs. Horton was quietly reading on one of the benches. Sunny Boy turned his head. Where was Joe?

"Looking for the boy that was swinging you?" demanded a girl in the next swing. "He ran off. I saw him going across the park after he gave you that one good push. Was he your brother? Did he get mad at you?"

Sunny Boy shook his head. He got out of the swing with some difficulty and trotted over to his mother.

"Joe Brown's gone," he announced mournfully. "Maybe he was mad 'cause I didn't swing him."

Mrs. Horton closed her magazine.

"Joe gone?" she echoed. "Oh, I'm so sorry! No, precious, I don't think he was hurt because you didn't swing him. I'm afraid he didn't want to go up to the hotel with us and see Daddy. I hate to think of a boy his age all alone in New York."

However, Joe had gone, and they could not hope to find him. Sunny Boy and Mother walked a bit about the pretty rocky paths and peeped into one or two of the little rustic cabins they found perched in unexpected places, and then Mother glanced at her watch and said it was time to go home.

"Are you tired, dear?" she asked as they started to walk to the nearest entrance.

"I guess my feet are," confided Sunny Boy. "They trip."

They saw one other thing that interested them very much before they left the park.

"What's that mon'ment?" Sunny Boy asked suddenly, pointing to a tall shaft that ended in a point at the top.

"That's the Egyptian obelisk," returned Mrs. Horton. "Come and look at it, dear. It is called 'Cleopatra's Needle,' and was brought all the way from Egypt. It is very, very old."

"How old?" demanded Sunny Boy practically. "It looks all right, Mother."

"Well, I've read that it was erected in Cairo, Egypt, sixteen hundred years before the birth of Christ," said Mrs. Horton. "So you see, dear, we are looking at a stone that is more than three thousand years old."

They took a surface car down to the hotel, and Sunny Boy, who did not like to say he was tired, was glad to curl up in a chair and look at a book till Daddy and Mother were ready to go to dinner.

Everyone went to bed early that night, for Mr. Horton had had a busy day, too, and was tired. He was not able to go about with them the next day, but on the following Monday he took them over to the Brooklyn Navy Yard and Sunny Boy actually went on board a battleship. The afternoon of the same day they crossed the wonderful Brooklyn Bridge and, getting out of the trolley car half way over, saw New York City from the middle of the river.

"See the ferryboats!" cried Sunny Boy, peering down into the water. "And there are, too, horses on 'em, just like the man said. Daddy, when can we go on a ferryboat?"

"That isn't so much to do," teased Mr. Horton. "I suppose we might go to-morrow. Olive, had you anything else planned?"

Mrs. Horton smiled and said that she had nothing in view more important than the ferryboat trip, so Sunny Boy went to bed that night to dream of riding a horse about the roof of a ferryboat while the Navy Yard band played and Joe Brown kept time like the band master.

CHAPTER VIII
THE FERRYBOAT RIDE

"**L**et's go away up front, Daddy, right up near the gate, so's I can see everything," suggested Sunny Boy eagerly, as he and Mother and Daddy entered the Twenty-third Street ferry house.

"All right. But let me get the tickets," said Mr. Horton, feeling in his pocket for change.

Sunny Boy was so short that he walked under the turnstile instead of through it, and the ticket man laughed when he saw him do it.

"Look out one of the sea gulls doesn't take you for a bite of breakfast," he called jokingly after him.

"Huh," Sunny Boy said resentfully to Mother, "I'm not so little. I know lots of children littler than I am. Wonder what he'd say if he saw Lottie Saunders going through his gate."

Lottie Saunders was a little friend of Sunny Boy's at home. She was not quite three years old.

There was a crowd of people waiting to get on the ferryboat and for a few minutes the Hortons had to stand at the closed door while the people on the boat walked off. There were a great many automobiles and horses and wagons and trucks coming off, too, and the drivers did a deal of shouting.

"Everybody's in a hurry," observed Sunny Boy, when the door was at last slid back and the crowd started to jostle its way on board.

Crowds are always in a hurry, if you have noticed it. They run and push and scramble to get somewhere, and then, when they are there, they sit down and rest or stand about contentedly, quite as though they did not know what hurrying meant.

"What do they do with the ropes?" asked Sunny Boy, as they went down the inclined plank and stepped on the ferryboat deck.

"They're what hold the boat in the slip," explained Mr. Horton. "If we stay on this back deck till the boat moves, you'll see the men take out those great hooks and wind the ropes on those wheels. Do you want to see them do it?"

Sunny Boy did, of course, and he waited till the gates were closed and the ropes loosened. Then two men, one on either side of the wharf, or slip, as they call the docks built for this kind of boat, gave a large spiked wheel one long, powerful turn, and it spun round rapidly, coiling up the ropes.

"Now we'll go up to the front," announced Mr. Horton, "and see what ails that noisy little tugboat we hear."

But Sunny Boy had made a discovery.

"Oh, Daddy!" he shouted. "There's a top! Let's go up!"

Mrs. Horton laughed.

"I'm sure Sunny will be an aviator when he grows up," she declared, smiling at her little boy. "He always wants to get as near to the sky as he can."

Sunny Boy was eager to climb the stairs to the second deck of the ferryboat, and he promised to help Mother up the stairs. So they went into the wide, pleasant cabin and up the broad staircase and came out on the sunny deck. There was a roof over it, and a cabin where people who did not like so much fresh air might sit, but Sunny Boy, of course, wanted to stand by the railing, and since it was a pleasant day, so did almost every one else.

"See the birds!" exclaimed Mrs. Horton, to whom a ferry trip was new too. "What do you suppose they find to eat?"

The gulls were flying gracefully above the water, sometimes coming close to the boat and now and then one would make a sudden dash down to the water, just dip his head in it and skim it with his wings, then soar up into the air again.

"I suppose they find bits of fruit and other refuse they can eat," replied Mr. Horton.

"That boat is going to run into the little flat one," said Sunny Boy positively, pointing an excited little forefinger at a fussy little tugboat making straight for a lazily floating barge loaded with coal.

"You watch," counseled Mr. Horton. "You can not see the rope because it is in the water, but that other tug up ahead is towing the barge. She'll have it out of the way before the other boat gets there."

And the towing tug did just that, apparently without hurrying, and before the noisy tugboat reached the coal barge it drifted safely out of the way.

"Now you can see where we are going in," said Mr. Horton, pointing out a dark opening just ahead of them.

The slips were made like stalls, with piling driven down on either side, and beams nailed across them. As the ferryboat turned into her slip she bumped smartly against the sides of the slip two or three times. It swayed, and Sunny Boy thought that there had been an accident.

"Oh, that often happens," his father assured them, as they stood a little to one side watching the people streaming off. "Sometimes, when it is very foggy, the boats have great difficulty in getting in, and sometimes an unusually high tide makes it hard for them, too."

The Hortons did not get off the ferryboat, and it was not long before more people were crowding on the decks again.

"Are they the same ones?" asked Sunny, puzzled.

"My no," answered Daddy quickly. "There are large cities on this side of the river, and people go back and forth between New York and New Jersey all day long. But I thought we were taking this trip because you wanted to see the horses enjoying a boat ride. Don't you want to go downstairs and look around?"

Sunny Boy said he did, and they went down.

"He looks like one of Grandpa's horses," said Sunny Boy, indicating a bay horse attached to a light delivery wagon. "Do you suppose he likes to go on a boat, Mother?"

"Sure he does," replied the driver, who had overheard. "He likes to go anywhere he doesn't have to use his own feet. That's what makes him so fat."

Sunny Boy laughed, and a colored man driving a team of horses harnessed to a wagon-load of empty barrels, rolled his eyes in delight.

"You've said it," he cackled joyously. "Dat horse sure look like he wished he was a automobile."

As the ferryboat drew near the New York side, Sunny Boy saw the wonderful "sky line" which is famous all over the world—the outline made by the tall buildings against the sky. Even a little boy could appreciate the picture the tall skyscrapers made, some buildings white, some gray, with here and there a gleaming gold dome against the fleecy September clouds.

"What makes the boat go?" Sunny Boy thought to ask, as the gates were opened and they were moving off with the crowd.

"Engines and steam," answered Mr. Horton. "And turn around and you'll see who steered us."

Sunny Boy turned and saw a white-bearded, blue-capped man in a small round pilot house above the deck. There was a wheel beside him which he turned as he wanted the boat to go.

"We've been sailing on the what is its name, Daddy?" asked Sunny, noticing for the first time large gold lettering below the pilot house which he guessed to be the name of the boat.

"The 'Lansdowne'," answered Mr. Horton. "And a nice old ferryboat she is. I don't know how you feel, Sunny, but I've had enough traveling for a few hours. Can't we have lunch down town, Olive?"

"And not go up to the hotel?" said Mrs. Horton. "Why, I'm willing. I know where I want to take Sunny Boy this afternoon, if you are going up to Yonkers to meet that buyer from Chicago."

"Where?" demanded Sunny Boy eagerly. "Where are we going, Mother?"

Mrs. Horton smiled mysteriously.

"Let it be a surprise," she suggested. "You're having so many good times, Sunny, that I'm afraid you'll find it hard to settle down and go to school when we are home again."

"School!" That made Sunny Boy jump. But just then Daddy hailed a street car, which they got on, and Sunny forgot everything else.

They found a clean, comfortable restaurant after a short ride on the street car, and Sunny Boy was quiet and good while Daddy looked over some papers and Mother read a letter from Aunt Bessie she had been carrying in her purse since breakfast time that morning.

"Bessie says," Mrs. Horton announced, "that some boy threw a ball through the front window and she's had it fixed. And Ruth and Nelson Baker send their love to you, Sunny. This is a very short letter because Aunt Bessie wants us to try to match the sample of silk she encloses and she hurried the letter to catch the next mail."

"I wonder if Nelson got the postal I sent him?" speculated Sunny Boy. "It was a picture of Central Park."

"He probably received it, and you'll see it in Ruth's album when you get home," said Mrs. Horton. "And now, Daddy, how about going uptown?"

Sunny Boy was excited, and wouldn't you be, if you were going somewhere you didn't know about, to see something no one had told you you would see? He wondered if they could be going to another menagerie, or if they were going shopping again.

"Wait and see," was all Mrs. Horton would answer, when he teased her.

They took the surface car, and after a few blocks Mr. Horton left them to get a train for Yonkers, which is a suburb of New York. Sunny Boy and his mother continued some half dozen blocks further and then left the car. They walked over a busy street, and suddenly Mrs. Horton stopped in front of a building with many entrances, and people crowding into them all.

"I know!" shouted Sunny Boy, as he saw a red and yellow poster. "It's a theater!"

"Yes, it is," admitted Mrs. Horton smiling. "I read in the paper last night that there was a children's matinee to-day, and Daddy 'phoned downstairs after you were asleep and bought our tickets. Can you tell what the play is, dear, from the pictures? See, here is a case of photographs."

Sunny Boy plunged his hands deep into his pockets, spread his feet sturdily apart, and studied the pictures seriously.

"There's a girl," he murmured aloud. "An' an old lady—she's a witch, I guess. Do I know it, Mother?"

"I've read you the story," said Mrs. Horton. "Don't you remember Snow White and the dwarfs?"

Sunny Boy remembered the story, and he would have liked to look at the photographs again, but Mrs. Horton thought it was time to go in and find their seats. An usher, a pretty girl, took them easily and quickly to the right row, and Sunny Boy found himself seated next to an elderly lady, with two children, a boy and a girl, evidently her grandchildren, in two seats directly in front of her.

"Why don't they sit next to her?" Sunny Boy whispered, watching the lady standing up to smooth out the little girl's hair-ribbon.

"They probably couldn't get three seats together," explained Mrs. Horton. "Better let me hold your hat, precious; you might drop it and some one would walk on it."

The orchestra was playing a gay bit of music, and Sunny's feet kept time to it merrily. He had been to the theater once or twice at home, generally at Christmas time, but this was decidedly different.

"I like New York," he confided to Mother.

The grandmotherly lady smiled.

"So you don't live here?" she asked pleasantly. "I have lived here so many years that no other place would seem like home. But Louise and David, my grandchildren, are, like you, visitors. They come from Georgia."

Mrs. Horton leaned forward.

"We're from Centronia," she volunteered, for Sunny Boy was too shy to do more than smile at the two children who had turned around when they heard their names spoken, and now grinned at him politely over the backs of their seats. "I don't believe Sunny Boy knows where Georgia is — do you, dear?"

"It's down South," said the little girl. "We slept on the train. And David was sick. I wasn't. Grandmother said he prob'ly ate too much ice-cream for his supper."

"Sh!" cautioned their grandmother. "The curtain's going up in a minute."

The lights went out, the music stopped, and Sunny Boy snuggled close to Mother. Slowly, oh, very slowly, the big blue curtain began to roll up, and the play began.

"Such a mean old stepmother," scolded Sunny Boy, at the end of the first act. "Poor little Snow White! I hope they never find out where she went when she ran away."

The orchestra played again, and then stopped as the lights were turned off for the second act. Sunny Boy gave a nervous little squeak as the curtain rose and he saw the dwarfs in their house.

CHAPTER IX
WHEN MAKE-BELIEVE IS REAL

T he dwarfs trotted gaily about the stage and finally went off to their work of chopping wood in the forest, leaving Snow White singing happily and brushing up the hearth.

"Isn't she pretty?" whispered Sunny Boy to Mother, who nodded and handed him the opera glasses.

Sunny Boy couldn't make the glasses work very well, but he loved to try, and he never felt that he was really at the theater unless he spent some minutes trying to look through the end that brought the stage nearer to him. He pretended that he had seen Snow White by the aid of the dainty pearl-handled glasses that were a gift from Daddy to Mother, and gave them back.

"Oh, look!" he nudged Mother sharply.

A queer old beggar woman had thrust her face close to the window in the dwarf's house and was watching Snow White.

"Sh!" whispered Mother, as Sunny Boy bounced in his seat. "You must keep still, dear. Don't make a noise."

The play went on, and Snow White let the old beggar woman in. She was selling apples, and right away, if you had been in the audience, you would have known she wasn't a beggar woman at all, but the wicked stepmother, who was also a witch.

"What did she say?" whispered Sunny Boy, who couldn't hear every word that was said on the stage.

"She wants to sell Snow White an apple, and Snow White says she has no money," explained Mother, in a low voice so that the people sitting near them would not be disturbed. "Now listen, and you'll hear what they say next."

Snow White had picked up her broom again and was going to work.

"I'll give you this beautiful apple," smiled the crafty old beggar woman. "See, my dear, I have it for you as a gift. Isn't it beautiful?"

She put it on the table, and went limping out of the door, pretty little Snow White running after her to thank her. At the window she stopped once, waved her hand, and vanished.

Snow White picked up the apple, and admired it. It was very red, and large and shining.

This was too much for Sunny Boy. He had kept still when Snow White let the witch in the door—"after the dwarfs told her not to let any one in the house, too," he grumbled as he watched her do it— and he had kept still while the witch tried to persuade her to buy an apple; but it was altogether too much to expect him to sit quietly there and watch Snow White eat that apple. Not for nothing had Harriet read him his book of fairy tales!

Snow White shook back her curly black hair and raised the apple to her rosy mouth for a bite.

"Don't eat it!" shouted Sunny Boy "at the top of his lungs" Harriet would have said. "Don't bite it! Throw it away! The witch poisoned it!"

He stood up on the seat, waving his hands frantically, a conspicuous little figure in a blue and white sailor suit.

How the people about him laughed! The lady sitting next to him had to wipe her eyes because she laughed so hard the tears came. Mother pulled Sunny Boy down into the seat beside her, and Snow White went on eating her apple, because, of course, the play had to go on.

"It's only make-believe, dear," whispered Mother, smoothing Sunny Boy's tousled hair. "You know she won't really die."

Sunny Boy smiled, a faint little smile.

"I guess I forgot it wasn't real," he said sheepishly. "Anyway, the little girl from Georgia is crying. I guess she forgot, too."

The little girl from Georgia was crying, the big tears rolling slowly and silently down her cheeks. Many of the children all over the house were crying, or if not actually crying, sniffling a bit. Snow White had eaten her apple and fallen asleep and the poor little brown dwarfs came home to find her, as they supposed, dead.

But the third and last act had a happy ending. Snow White came to life again, and the big curtain came down and the lights flared up to show a houseful of happy, smiling children being buttoned into coats and gloves, and having their caps and hats and bonnets put on for them by mothers and grandmothers and aunts and big sisters.

Sunny Boy walked soberly up the aisle beside his mother, thinking about a great many things. He thought about the dwarfs, and how he would like to know some to play with. He thought about the big theater, and wondered if it was fun to be an actor. And then he thought what a lot of children had come to see the play, and whether they all lived in New York. He put this last thought into words.

"Do they all live here?" he asked Mother, who, of course, did not know what he had been thinking and had to have it explained to her.

"No, I don't suppose they all live here," she said thoughtfully, when Sunny Boy had told her. "I imagine a great many of these boys and girls are New Yorkers and live in the houses and apartments we have seen in the city. Some of them, I am sure, come from the suburban towns to the matinee, the way the children from Glendale come in to Centronia when we have a good play at our theaters, you know. And some of these children you saw this afternoon are like a little boy I know—they come from other cities on their first visit to New York. Though not all of them stand up and shout at the stage people, I'm glad to say."

Sunny Boy snickered.

"Well, next time I won't," he promised. "Won't Daddy laugh when I tell him? Guess he'll think I never went to the theater."

Daddy did laugh when they told him that night, after they had had dinner and were up in their room together. Sunny Boy had had his bath and, all cool and clean, was curled up in his pink pajamas in a blanket on Mother's bed trying to keep awake and listen to Mother and Daddy talk.

"Right out loud in the theater!" repeated Mr. Horton, pretending to be shocked. "Why, Sunny Boy, you must be more careful. I don't suppose you stopped to think that if Snow White had taken your advice and thrown away the apple, the rest of the play couldn't have happened."

"Yes, and suppose they had come down to you and had said you would have to write them a new fairy story before they could finish the play," teased Mrs. Horton. "What would you have done then, Sunny?"

"I'd have just said I couldn't," giggled Sunny Boy, trying to turn a summersault on the bed.

"Some one called you up about five o'clock this afternoon," said Mr. Horton, speaking to his wife. "It was a short time before you came in. She said she would call again after dinner."

"I didn't know I knew any one in New York, at least any one who knew we were here," Mrs. Horton began, puzzled, when the telephone on the table rang.

She went to answer it, and Sunny Boy and Daddy had a pillow fight, which was all the more exciting because they had to keep quiet and not bother Mother at the telephone. Sunny Boy grew red in the face, not daring to laugh aloud, and Daddy tickled him unmercifully.

"There, now, do be still," said Mrs. Horton, hanging up the receiver and coming over to the bed where Sunny Boy and his father were rolling around, each apparently trying to stuff a pillow down the other's neck. "Harry! Sunny! Neither of you will go to sleep to-night. Sunny Boy and I are invited to pay a call to-morrow afternoon."

"All right, let's." A flushed and triumphant Sunny Boy sat up and smiled blissfully at his mother. He had had "last whack" at Daddy, who was now busy brushing lint off his trousers.

Mrs. Horton laughed.

"Sunny, you're getting to be keen for going," she declared. "You don't seem to care where you go as long as it is somewhere. I'm anxious to see you in school and having a little less excitement. And look at my bed!"

"That's all right," Mr. Horton assured her hastily. "We scoop Sunny Boy off so." He swung Sunny high in the air and landed him safely in his own little bed. "Then we pat up the pillows, so, and smooth the covers like this—and there you are!"

"Thank you," smiled Mrs. Horton. "Who do you suppose called me up?"

Mr. Horton couldn't guess, and Sunny Boy couldn't guess.

"Adele Parker," announced Mrs. Horton. "We went to school together, but I haven't seen her since she was married. Bessie and her younger sister are great chums, and Bessie wrote the sister we were in New York. She gave our address and Adele has hunted us up. She wants me to come up to-morrow afternoon. They are just back from the country, and the house is all torn up, so we won't stay long. But I do want to see her."

Sunny Boy dropped asleep while they were talking, and in the morning he and Mother went shopping again, because Daddy was to have an all-day conference with business men and they must amuse themselves.

"I think we ought to choose a few little gifts to take to the friends at home," suggested Mrs. Horton, as she and Sunny Boy stepped from the car and went into one of the beautiful big shops. "Daddy says we won't be here much longer, perhaps not more than another week. Wouldn't you like to take something home to Nelson and Ruth?"

Sunny Boy thought this would be very nice, but what should he take them?

"Well, suppose you think about it, while I buy some things for Aunt Bessie and Aunt Betty Martinson and Harriet," said Mrs. Horton.

Sunny Boy puzzled and puzzled, but Mother was all through her shopping before he could think of a single thing that Ruth and Nelson might like.

"Could we buy 'em a spress wagon?" he asked doubtfully. "Nelson's always borrowing mine. Or roller skates?"

"Dear me," said Mrs. Horton, "don't you think something we could pack in the trunk would be nicer? It needn't be a large gift, you know. Just something they can say came from New York. We'll go up to the toy department and look around."

This was a different shop from the first one they had visited, and Sunny Boy had to see all the toys before he could settle down to choosing gifts for Ruth and Nelson. Finally, by Mother's advice, he settled on a quaint little painted music box for Ruth that played four different tunes, and a picture puzzle game for Nelson, who liked to put things together. These were sent home to the hotel so that Sunny Boy and Mother would not have to carry packages with them the rest of the day.

"Now we'll go to the restaurant and have lunch," planned Mrs. Horton, leading the way to the elevator. "And then I want to get a box of nice candy to take Adele's children. I hope their mother lets them eat candy."

"Will there be some children?" asked Sunny Boy, surprised. "That will be fun. Houses where I sit on a chair visiting are kind of lonesome."

"I don't doubt it," agreed Mother sympathetically. "Well, you'll find three children to visit with this afternoon. You must have been asleep last night when I told Daddy. Adele Parker has two boys and a little girl."

"Daddy calls her Mrs. Kennedy," objected Sunny Boy, following Mother out of the elevator into a large dining room.

Mrs. Horton stopped at the door till the waitress should find them seats.

"She is Mrs. Kennedy," Mother admitted, smiling. "I call her Adele Parker because that was her name when I knew her at school. She probably calls me Olive Andrew, because that was my name before it was Mrs. Horton."

The waitress came up to them and beckoned.

"There's a table for two over by the window," she said. "I'll see that some one takes your order."

CHAPTER X
MORE SIGHTSEEING

S unny Boy and Mother had a pleasant lunch, Sunny Boy, as he ate his sandwiches and drank his milk, looking down into the street six or seven stories below, or out over the roofs of the city.

"Now we're going to Adele's," he remarked, as Mother gathered up her gloves and purse.

"Oh, Sunny Boy!" Mrs. Horton surveyed him half laughingly, half with despair. "You musn't call her Adele. Say Mrs. Kennedy. You never call Mother's friends by their first names, you know you don't."

"Well, I don't know her," offered Sunny Boy mildly, as though that made a difference.

They took a bus, which never lost its charm for Sunny, and after a rather long ride, got out at a cross street and walked until they reached a narrow, five-storied brick house with gay window boxes at every window. A maid opened the door for them and showed them into a pleasant, rather small room where a little girl sat at the grand piano, practicing.

She glanced up shyly as Mrs. Horton and Sunny Boy came in.

"I'm sure I know who you are," smiled Mrs. Horton. "You must be Alice."

The little girl got up and made a pretty curtsy.

"I'm Alice Kennedy," she said, smiling too. "Are you Mother's friend, Mrs. Horton? Is he your little boy?"

Mrs. Kennedy came in as Mrs. Horton nodded, and there was a great showering of kisses and many questions asked and ever so many introductions, for two small boys followed Mrs. Kennedy in and they were presented as her sons, Dick and Paul.

"Now you and I'll go upstairs where it is cozier," said Mrs. Kennedy, when every one knew every one else, "and the children shall take Sunny Boy up to their playroom on the top floor."

"We brought a little candy," explained Mrs. Horton, giving Sunny Boy the box. "Are you willing to have it passed?"

Mrs. Kennedy was, so each of the children had three pieces and climbed the stairs to the playroom chattering like old friends.

"Have you been to the ac-quarium?" asked Paul, pronouncing it as if it were two words. He was rocking Sunny Boy on his rocking horse, which was as large as a small pony and had real hair in its mane and tail.

"Got one at home," announced Sunny Boy contentedly. "There were ten goldfish but one died."

"Oh, Paul means the real aquarium," explained Alice. "Down at the Battery, with the queerest fish you ever saw, and big tanks, and corals, and everything."

No, Sunny Boy hadn't seen that. He was so much interested in Alice's descriptions that when the two mothers came up to see what they were doing, they found them still talking about the fish.

"Hasn't Sunny Boy been down to the Battery?" asked Mrs. Kennedy. "Why, we must all go. How about to-morrow?"

Mrs. Horton explained that she had planned to go to the Statue of Liberty the following day.

"You can do that easily in the afternoon," said Mrs. Kennedy. "We might as well make a day of it. I have to get the children ready for school, and one day is all I can spare. Suppose we meet at the Battery in the morning and see the aquarium. We'll have lunch somewhere and take the boat right from the Battery for Bedloe's Island."

So it was arranged that they should meet the next morning, and Sunny Boy and Mother went back to the hotel to tell Daddy all about their plans and to hear about his busy day.

As soon as Sunny Boy and Mother entered the park at the Battery the following morning, the glint of water in the sun attracted him.

"Why is it the Battery?" he asked. "Are there guns?"

"There used to be," said Mother. "Long ago, when instead of a park, this end of New York was high rocks, a water battery guarded the town and was used a little in the Revolution. That is where the Battery gets its name. The aquarium is housed in the old fort."

"I see Alice," cried Sunny Boy.

"Yes, here they all are," said Mother.

The Kennedy family came up to them, and together they walked toward the dingy building where the queer fish, Sunny had been told, lived.

"It doesn't look much, but think who's been in it," remarked Alice. She went to school and liked history. "After it stopped being a fort, they called it Castle Garden, and three presidents of the United States held receptions there. 'Sides Lafayette landed there when he came to this country to visit. Didn't he, Mother?"

"Yes," agreed Mrs. Kennedy. "But I think Sunny Boy is more interested just now in seeing the fish. Here we are, and please, children, don't all talk at once and do try to keep together."

Sunny Boy stared about him in amazement. Huge glass tanks with the queerest fish he had ever seen swimming in them were on all sides of him. A sudden noise, like a harsh cough, startled him.

"That's a seal," laughed Dick. "Come on over here, Sunny, and see them."

Funny, flat heads, bright eyes and "whiskers" had the seals, and they made the queer coughing sound Sunny Boy had heard. He privately didn't think they were very pretty, and he admired the great turtles in another tank much more.

"Let's go in back and see if we can touch the fish," he suggested to Dick, when they had seen all the open tanks on the floor. "I'd like to look out from behind there and see how it seems."

Dick was puzzled, but Alice understood right away.

"Those are all tanks, with just glass in front," she informed Sunny Boy.

The round walls of the fort were set with what looked like glass plates, behind which great lazy fish were idly swimming. It looked as though one could go in back of them and see through, and perhaps touch the fish in the water.

After they had seen all the fish in all the tanks downstairs, they went upstairs and looked at the fish and the corals and anemones and funny crabs living and growing in other glass tanks. The anemones looked like beautiful, vivid flowers, and Mrs. Horton and Mrs. Kennedy both exclaimed over their beauty.

"I like the crab that walks crooked best," announced Sunny Boy, and Dick and Paul agreed with him.

When they came out of the aquarium they walked about the picturesque old park a little, and then found a small place where they had lunch.

"What does Sunny Boy know about the statue we're going to see?" asked Mrs. Kennedy, as they stepped on board the boat that was to take them to the Statue of Liberty that afternoon. "My children have been so often that it is an old story to them."

"I know," cried Sunny Boy eagerly. "Donald Joyce told me. I know, don't I, Mother?"

"Donald Joyce is a young neighbor of ours who went to war and came back safely," said Mrs. Horton.

"An' Donald said," recited Sunny Boy, slowly and carefully because he did not want to forget before he had told it all, "the Statue of Liberty was made by a man—you say it, Mother," he broke off. "It begins with 'B'."

"A man named Bartholdi," said Mrs. Horton smilingly.

"A man named Bartholdi," repeated Sunny Boy. "He came over from France to see us, and he saw all the im-im-immigrants acting glad when they first saw the United States. So he went home and asked the French to give some money so's he could build us a statue. And they did. And Bartholdi made the statue and it's a present from France. Donald Joyce said the soldiers were awful glad to see it when they came home from France and they were glad they'd helped fight for the country that made the Statue of Liberty, too."

"Isn't that nice?" said Alice Kennedy, with satisfaction. "I never heard that part about the soldiers being glad. The boat's moving, Sunny!"

The four children hung over the rail, pulled back now and then by an anxious mother, during the short sail. Alice had brought some crumbs of bread with her, and they amused themselves by throwing these into the water for the gulls.

"See the boats!" cried Sunny Boy, pointing to several large steamers plainly seen from their boat.

"That's Ellis Island we're passing," explained Mrs. Kennedy. "All the immigrants are sent there from the ships on which they arrive. They see the Statue of Liberty first, Sunny, as you said."

The beautiful bronze Statue of Liberty, familiar to all the boys and girls of our country through pictures if not by actual sight, loomed up before the passengers on the boat now. It was so much larger than Sunny Boy had expected, that he stared at it silently.

"The torch isn't lit, but you can imagine how wonderful it must look then," said Mrs. Horton, as the boat docked and the people prepared to go ashore. "Just think of the millions of people who have been glad to catch their first glimpse of 'Miss Liberty'."

"It's awful big," Sunny managed to gasp.

"Guess how high it is," said Alice. "You can't? Well, it's one hundred and fifty-one feet high. My father told me. And that's not counting the thing it stands on."

"Don't talk all the time, Alice," implored her mother. "Let Sunny Boy have time to collect his thoughts. Shall we walk around it first, dear, before we go in?"

They walked slowly around the statue, and then went inside.

"Now we'll go up," chattered Alice. "I just love going up and looking out over the bay when we get there."

Sunny Boy planted his feet firmly on the stone floor.

"I isn't going up," he announced quietly.

"Why, Sunny! Why not? Don't you want to?" several voices urged him at once.

Sunny Boy shook his head.

"I'll wait for you," he said politely.

"But we've been up," declared Dick and Paul. "Nobody ever comes 'way out to the Island and not go up. What will people say?"

"You haven't seen the Statue of Liberty at all," cried Alice, greatly disappointed.

"I'd rather not," insisted Sunny Boy.

The two mothers looked at each other and laughed.

"I went up with Harry years ago," said Mrs. Horton. "Of course I should like Sunny Boy to have the experience, but he'll come to New York other times I hope. Anyway, I can't agree with Alice that he hasn't seen the statue. He can learn the dimensions when he studies arithmetic."

Sunny Boy wasn't quite sure in his own mind why he refused to take the elevator, as people all around him were doing, and go to the top of the statue. He only knew that he would be dreadfully unhappy if any one made him go.

He was very quiet on the trip back, but all the children were a little tired from their busy day and not so inclined to be hilarious as earlier in the afternoon. They all said good-bye to Sunny Boy at the ferry, for the Kennedys took a different way from Sunny Boy and his mother.

"We're going home in the subway," said Mrs. Kennedy, kissing Mrs. Horton. "It's the quickest way to travel. I think you're foolish to drag Sunny around on the surface cars."

"I want to wait till his father can go with us," answered Mrs. Horton. "Your noisy old subways make me nervous, Adele."

Sunny Boy, sleepily leaning against Mother's shoulder in the crowded street car, remembered this.

"What's a subway?" he asked drowsily. "Where is it, Mother?"

"You'll find out perhaps to-morrow, if Daddy isn't too busy," Mother assured him. "Oh, precious, see this poor old woman."

Sunny Boy sat up, wide awake instantly.

An old woman, bent and lame, had entered the car and stood swaying, trying to reach a hanger. She had a worn old shawl over her shoulders and carried a big basket.

Sunny Boy slipped out of his place.

"Here's a seat for you," he called clearly.

The woman sat down heavily, mumbling her thanks, and Sunny Boy had to stand the rest of the way home. Not that he minded. For one thing, it kept him wide awake, and for another, his father always gave every woman his seat in a crowded car, and Sunny Boy was sure he would be glad to hear that Sunny Boy had done the same.

"And what do we do to-morrow?" this same Daddy asked that night as he helped a very tired, sleepy little boy to get ready for bed. "I'm going to play with you and Mother all day, you know."

Sunny Boy was ready with his reply.

"To-morrow," he said indistinctly, in the midst of a big yawn, "we're going to travel quick on the subway!"

CHAPTER XI
SUNNY BOY GETS LOST

"**D**o you remember when you were counting up the kinds of cars you had ridden on?" asked Daddy, as he and Sunny Boy stood on the walk waiting for Mother, who had gone into a drugstore to buy some postage stamps.

Sunny Boy nodded.

"Well, the subway is one kind you haven't been on," said Daddy.

Sunny Boy was surprised.

"But it isn't cars, Daddy," he argued. "I think it is a boat."

Mr. Horton laughed.

"The subway isn't what you ride on," he tried to explain. "It's what you ride *in*. The trains go through the subway, Sunny."

Mrs. Horton came out with her postage stamps just then, and the three walked till they came to one of the funny little houses Sunny Boy had seen at many street corners. Mr. Horton led the way straight down the steps.

"Why, we're going down cellar!" exclaimed the astonished little boy, who followed him. "Daddy, do the trains run in the cellar?"

It was clear that they did, for even before they reached the last step the rumble and roar of a coming train was heard. It was light and bright in the subway station, and Sunny Boy thought that it did not seem like a cellar at all.

He stood as close to the edge of the platform as his father would let him and peered up the track. It was dark, like a tunnel, and colored lights winked at him from the walls.

"Will the next be our train?" he asked.

"We can take any that comes," answered Daddy. "This is an express station. See the red light coming—that is a train."

A tiny red glow far in the distance grew larger and larger, and the roar and rumble of the train was heard. A long train of cars, brilliantly lighted, swept past them, such a long train that Sunny Boy thought at first that it was not going to stop. But it did.

"Where's the engine?" he asked disappointedly, as he and Mother and Daddy stepped on through a center door.

"There isn't any engine," replied his father. "Don't you remember the elevated train has no engine, either? Both kinds of trains are run by electricity. If Mother doesn't mind, we'll go up in the first car and watch from the front door."

Mrs. Horton didn't mind, even though they had to walk almost the length of the train to reach the first car. There were plenty of seats in this car, and Mrs. Horton sat down to rest while Sunny Boy and his father stood at the door and peered through the glass panel. They could see the tracks stretching ahead of them, and as they watched the train flashed through a station without stopping.

Sunny Boy was delighted.

"Let's ride all day," he suggested. "Don't get off, Daddy. See the blue light! What's that for?"

Mr. Horton didn't know. It was some sort of signal for the engineer. The engineer was shut away from them in a little enclosed corner space where it was dark and he could see the lights ahead of him plainly.

When they stopped at a station, many people always got off, but seemingly as many crowded on.

"Where are we going, Daddy?" Sunny Boy thought to ask at one of these stops.

"A long way," Daddy assured him. "Up to Bronx Park and the Zoological Garden. I thought you'd like to see the animals."

Sunny Boy was fond of animals, but he was sure that he would never again have as much fun as he was having watching the train speed along those dark shining rails.

"You can go and sit down, if you're tired, Daddy," he told his father. "I can stay here alone."

Mr. Horton did go back and sit down beside Mother.

"I guess maybe I will sit down a minute," said Sunny Boy, after he had stood up for many blocks. "I'm not tired, but my feet are."

Then, before his feet were rested, Daddy announced that the next station was theirs. They were out of the subway now, riding along in the open air, and he took Mother's hand.

"And now," said Mr. Horton, with a smile for Sunny as they left the train and, after a short walk, entered the park, "let's see everything!"

This they proceeded to do.

There isn't room to tell you of the wonderful animals they saw, the buffaloes, the beautiful deer, so tame that they came up to the wires to have their noses rubbed; of the lions and tigers and panthers and leopards; of strange animals that Sunny Boy had never seen even in his book of wild animals; and of the woods where they enjoyed their lunch, just as if they were on a picnic. They visited the Botanical Gardens, too, where Mother made as much fuss over the flowers as Sunny Boy had over the baby deer, and where Daddy took pictures of them both to send to Grandpa and Grandma Horton.

"We may be tired," Daddy admitted, when he looked at his watch and found it was time for them to go home, "but then look what we have for being tired!"

Sunny Boy was busy thinking of all the things he had seen, and he forgot to be disappointed because the first car was full and he couldn't get near the door to look out, as he had coming up that morning.

"We'll change at Forty-second Street," he heard Daddy say to Mother. "I'm afraid we stayed a little too long and will be caught in the rush."

Mrs. Horton had a seat, but Sunny Boy and Daddy were standing.

"Hang on to my coat sleeve and you'll be steady enough," Daddy advised his little son.

"I think it would be better if he sat in his mother's lap, don't you?" said Mrs. Horton, smiling.

"But I'm not slipping, Mother," he announced proudly. "Wouldn't you think I was standing without holding on to anything?"

"You manage very nicely," Mrs. Horton told him. "Isn't the next stop ours, Harry?"

It was, and Mr. Horton had to elbow a little path for them to the door, there were so many people trying to get in and out at the same time. Sunny Boy had hold of Mother's dress, and as they squeezed out of the car he lost his grasp.

"Goodness," he scolded, "I should think folks would wait a minute. That man bumped right into me and never said 'excuse me.'"

Sunny Boy looked ahead and saw Mother's blue dress and tan coat.

"I 'spect I'd better hurry," he said aloud.

He ran after the blue dress and tan coat and slipped in through a door just a second before the guard closed it.

Then Sunny Boy made a surprising discovery.

The blue dress and the tan coat were not Mother's at all! He had followed a strange woman!

He looked all around the car and couldn't see his own mother, nor a sign of Daddy. Though Sunny Boy did not know it, he had crossed the station platform and taken an uptown train. He was riding away from the hotel as fast as the noisy rumbling subway train could carry him.

"It's pretty crowded," said Sunny Boy to himself. "Maybe when some more folks get off at the next station, I can see Mother."

But though people got off at the next station and the next, there was no Mother.

Sunny Boy sat quietly. No one, looking at him, would have guessed that he was lost. When the crowd of people began to thin out, he followed a fat man with a big basket to the door and up the steps out into the street.

It was still light enough to see clearly, and Sunny Boy knew that he had never been in this part of New York. There were many small shops on either side of the street and moving picture places with great glaring signs already lit.

"Papers!" a boy on the corner was calling. "Papers!"

As Sunny watched him, several men stepped up and bought papers and ran down the subway steps.

Sunny felt in his pocket. There were two bright pennies there, slipped in by Mother, who always put money in the pocket of each new suit. Sunny jammed his hat more tightly on his yellow head and walked over to where the newsboy stood.

"Want a paper?" the boy grinned at him in a friendly way. "*World?* Well, didn't your father say? How much you got?"

Sunny Boy held out his pennies silently.

The boy whipped a paper from the pack under his arm, folded it neatly and gave it to Sunny, taking his money as he did so.

"You'd better scoot," he advised him kindly. "If your father's waiting for that paper he'll think you're reading it. Hurry up—get a move on!"

Sunny Boy sat down sociably on an old soap box.

"Daddy isn't waiting," he said.

"Papers! Here you are, sir!" the boy made change quickly with not too clean hands. "Then what do you want a paper for? You can't read, can you?"

"Well some writing I can," admitted Sunny Boy modestly. "That is, if it's printed. I thought maybe you'd talk to me."

"Talk to you!" repeated the newsboy. "Say, kid, you ought to be home running errands for supper."

Sunny Boy doubled a small foot under him.

"I got lost," he announced casually.

"Sunny Boy sat down sociably on an old soap box"

"In the subway. They pushed me and then I thought I saw mother and it was another lady."

The boy glanced at him sharply.

"You stringing me?" he demanded. "You do look as if you were used to having somebody around with you. Don't you know where you live?"

"Of course I do," declared Sunny Boy quickly. "I always 'member where I live. It's the Macnapin Hotel."

The newsboy had sold nearly all his papers now and he felt that he could take a little time to question this strange child who sat on the soap box and said he was lost.

"That's a new one to me," he admitted, when Sunny Boy mentioned the hotel. "Is it in New York?"

"My, yes!" Sunny Boy answered, surprised. "Don't you know? I know one of the bell-boys."

"Well, how do you get to it?" demanded the newsboy.

Sunny Boy didn't know.

"Well, then, what's your name?" said his new friend.

"Sunny Boy," came the prompt answer.

The newsboy laughed.

"'Sunny Boy'!" he jeered. "That's a great name to be lost with. S'pose your folks will put an ad in to-morrow's papers for a lost child named Sunny Boy?"

Now by this time Sunny was very hungry and tired from his long day at the Park. He was worried, too, and he felt very far away from his daddy and mother. Two big tears gathered in his eyes and ran down his face.

CHAPTER XII
SUNNY BOY IS FOUND

"O h, I say!" the newsboy's voice changed instantly. "Don't cry, kid. If you say your name is Sunny Boy, all right, it is. And I'll even have it you live at the Macnapin Hotel, though where that is is more than I know. Quit crying, I tell you; you're going home along with me."

Sunny Boy continued to stare at him, the tears slowly chasing down his cheeks.

"I want my mother!" he sobbed forlornly.

"All right, all right, I'll get her for you," promised the distracted older boy. "You leave it to Tim Harrity, and there won't nothing happen to you. Only quit crying, because folks are beginning to look at you. Come on. I'm through for the night."

Sunny Boy slipped a hot little hand into Tim's.

"Where we going?" he quavered.

"Home," said Tim Harrity briefly. "When I'm sold out, I go home. You come along now, and don't talk because I'm trying to figure out what hotel you belong at."

Sunny Boy trotted beside Tim, obediently silent. He was so tired that his feet stumbled, but he plodded on, keeping a tight clutch on his friend's hand.

Suddenly Tim stopped short and gave a shout.

"I have it!" he cried, snapping his fingers excitedly. "I'll bet what you're trying to say is the 'McAlpin'! Aren't you staying at the McAlpin Hotel?"

"Why, yes," admitted Sunny Boy, surprised. "I told you so."

Tim was in high good humor at his cleverness in solving the riddle, and he hurried Sunny Boy down the street as fast as he could go. Presently they came to a smaller street and turned the corner. The houses were very close together, and it seemed to Sunny that at least three people were hanging out of every window. Babies toddled all over the sidewalk, and in one place, where a pushcart had broken down, a swarm of little children quarreled over a heap of half-rotten pears.

"Here we are," announced Tim, steering Sunny Boy up the rickety steps of a sagging brick house. "Go careful, 'cause you're not used to the stairs. And don't take hold of the railing—it's weak."

Sunny Boy felt his way up three pairs of dark stairs behind Tim, and when they reached the third floor a door opened to let a flood of light out on them.

"That you, Tim?" some one called. "You're late. I set the stew back to keep it hot. Glory be, and who is it you're bringing home with you?"

Sunny Boy blinked. The room was hot and the glaring light blinded him. He was dizzily aware that a great many people stood around staring at him.

Tim pulled his hand free.

"The rest of you get back," he commanded his family sternly. "Where's Ma? This kid's lost, and if you don't want him crying again, keep away till Ma's had a chance to tell him what's what."

Then from out another room stepped a large woman with a great kind red face. She was drying her hands on her apron, and she had evidently been washing, for her purple wrapper was splashed with soap-suds. But her voice went right to Sunny's heart.

"Lost, is it?" she said tenderly. "Saints above, what a baby to be out alone in this city! An' his poor mother, the saints pity her she'll be that wild. There, there, dearie, you're all right. A bit of supper's what you're needin'. And then 'tis Timmie himself who shall be taking ye home."

She gathered Sunny Boy into her capacious lap and crooned over him in the deep rich voice that her own six children knew and loved without realizing its charm.

"'Tis a cruel city to the babies," she sighed, smoothing Sunny Boy's hair with a touch as gentle as that of his own mother's. "But your poor mother—the saints help her. Timmie, ye must not be waiting a minute. Come, Theresa, give him a sup of stew. We must be taking him home before the heart of the mother is broke entirely."

Tim, who had been noisily washing at the sink, was frowning into the cracked mirror above it as he tried to part his hair exactly in the center.

"I want to telephone first," he explained. "He's after giving me such a crazy name—Sunny Boy, I've doped it out that he belongs at the McAlpin Hotel, but there's no reason why I should make a fool of myself by taking him 'way down there and then being told that no child is lost from there."

A pretty, dark-haired girl, Sunny Boy called her a young lady in his mind, was stirring something at the stove. She wore a pink blouse and was smiling.

"I'll bring him some stew over there, Ma," she suggested. "The children have mussed up the table pretty well, and they'd take his appetite away with their eyes. Can't you stand back a bit?" she demanded of the four children, three little boys and a girl, who stood in a ring about Sunny Boy and their mother, gazing fixedly at the stranger.

"I'll eat first, I guess," decided Timmie. "I didn't get me a crumb of lunch, and after I've told his folks he's safe they'll be wanting to see him the next minute. Just give me a taste of the stew on some bread, Theresa."

Theresa had already taken her mother a plate for Sunny, and now she gave her brother his supper. The stew was hot and really delicious, and Sunny Boy was sure he had never tasted anything so good. Mrs. Harrity held the plate for him and patted him now and then as he ate. The Harrity children edged nearer and nearer, till a frown from their mother drove them back.

"Going now," announced Tim, seizing his cap.

He slammed the door with such force that the plates on the table rattled, but no one seemed to mind it. They could hear him cheerfully whistling as he clattered downstairs.

Theresa put some water on to heat for the dishes, and came over near her mother and Sunny Boy. She took the little girl on her lap.

"Timmie will help you all right," she assured Sunny Boy, nodding and smiling at him encouragingly. "Tim's a great lad for seeing things through. How did he come to find you?"

Sunny Boy explained.

"Well, well," said Mrs. Harrity. "If you're not used to it, the subway's built for confusin' ye. But Marty there, he's seven next birthday, he can get about as well as the next one."

Marty grinned and wriggled uneasily.

"I'm five," said Sunny Boy conversationally.

"Five now, well, well," repeated Mrs. Harrity. "Rose over there is five. Jim's eight and Thomas, he that's licking the gravy spoon, is nine. An' a fine, noisy bunch they do be. The kettle is boilin', Theresa."

Theresa put her little sister down, and rolling back the sleeves of her pink waist, began to gather up the dishes. Thomas had to be made to give up the gravy spoon, which he was apparently enjoying very much.

Theresa had just poured the water over the dishes in the pan and was folding up the tablecloth, when the noise of some one falling upstairs startled them.

"That's Timmie," declared Mrs. Harrity excitedly. "The boy's in such a hurry to tell his news he can't wait to walk. He'll be prayin' for wings. Open the door, Marty."

Tim dashed in, so out of breath that for several seconds he couldn't tell them the news. When he could speak, he fairly danced up and down, snapping his fingers at Sunny Boy to emphasize his words.

"It's all right!" he gasped. "I found 'em, Ma. They want me to bring Sunny Boy right down. They were just going to the police—seems they spent an hour or two riding up an' down in the subway looking for him and asking all the guards."

The Harritys had all gathered in a circle again.

"Let the kid breathe," protested Tim. "Say, Ma, I had a great time getting 'em. I called the hotel, and the switchboard operator thought I was stringing her. I knew that 'Sunny Boy' was a fool name to tell anybody, but when she got fresh I made her give me the clerk.

"'Has anybody down there lost a child?' I asks. 'There's a boy at my house says his name's Sunny Boy and he's lost.'"

"'Well, find out the rest of his name,' snaps the clerk. And say, young feller," Tim pretended to glare at Sunny Boy, "next time you get lost you want to have a name folks can get quicker than the one you're wearing now."

"Hurry up," urged Theresa impatiently. "Did you find his mother?"

"I'm hurrying," retorted Tim. "Leave a feller alone, can't you? I heard the clerk say to some one. 'Here's a nut says he has a lost child; you don't know anything about it, do you?'"

"I couldn't hear what the other one said, and then, all of a sudden, some one shouts. 'For the love of Pete, hold that wire! Are you dumb? The Hortons lost their kid in the subway coming down this afternoon.'"

"Then what happened?" asked Theresa.

"Nothing much," answered Tim, who like some other story tellers always stopped short when the story got exciting. "The clerk told me to hold the call, and I heard him ordering the girl to put me on another wire. A man answered, an' he didn't give me time to say more than 'Sunny Boy' when he sang out; 'All right, Mother, the boy's been found.' Then I told him where we were, and he says should he send a taxi, but I told him the subway'd make better time. We can take an express. And that's about all, I guess."

"Well you must be hurrying off," said Mrs. Harrity. "Let me polish his face a bit, so they won't think he's been neglected entirely, an' then the two of yese must be goin'. 'Tis glad I am that his mother won't have to live through a night wondering if harm's come to him."

Mrs. Harrity washed Sunny Boy's face and hands carefully and brushed his hair with a brush that was probably the family hairbrush and certainly showed signs of much use. She kissed him heartily when he was ready, and he put his arms about her neck and hugged her.

"Hurry up," urged Tim, pulling him toward the door. "Cut the good-byes short, for I can't be accused of wasting time on this trip."

"Tim," whispered Theresa, "Timmie, you sure you have enough?"

Tim rattled the change in his pockets by way of answer.

"Plenty," he said proudly. "I wasn't after giving Ma any to-night. When I come back I'll fix it up with her. We're off now—watch your step."

The whole Harrity family stood at the top of the stairs and watched them go down.

"Good-bye!" cried the children, losing their shyness as Sunny Boy went further away. "Good-bye, Sunny Boy!"

Sunny Boy waved his hand. Tim was hurrying him down so fast that he was in danger of tripping if he turned. At the very foot of the stairs he stopped and looked up. Mrs. Harrity was leaning over the railing.

"A blessin' on ye, darlin'," she called. "Good-bye."

CHAPTER XIII
HELPING THE HARRITYS

"**N**ow you hang on to me," commanded Tim, as he and Sunny Boy went down the subway steps into the warm, moist air of the station. "I don't aim to lose you changing, and we have to change, 'cause this ain't an express station."

Sunny Boy obediently "hung on to" Tim, keeping so close beside him that several times it was inconvenient, as when people tried to get past them at the door of the car. The train was crowded, and the two boys had to stand.

"We change here," warned Tim, when they reached the express station. "Look sharp!"

Sunny Boy breathed a sigh of relief when they were safely on the express train; he didn't trust himself to change cars.

"You look kind of beat out," commented Tim, eyeing his charge critically when they were near their last stop. "I s'pose you've done more going to-day than you're used to. Never mind, we're most there now.

"I wonder," Tim said, when they reached the entrance of the McAlpin Hotel a few minutes later, "will I have to go in and let that bunch look me over? I didn't bring my dress suit, and I ain't exactly crazy about giving 'em something to stare at."

Sunny Boy's little heart understood. Tim was ashamed of his shabby clothes, and he knew that the bright lights would make his worn coat reveal every spot and hole.

"Mother won't care," Sunny assured him. "Come on, Tim, I'll show you."

So it was Sunny Boy who pulled Tim into the foyer, and even then Tim would have backed out if, almost the instant they entered the door, some one had not come running to them.

"Oh, my baby!" cried Sunny Boy's mother, gathering him up and hugging him.

Tim felt a hand on his shoulder, and looked up to find Sunny Boy's father smiling down at him.

"You look as if you might cut and run," said Mr. Horton cheerfully. "And you and I must have a little talk first. Olive, here's the chap who found Sunny Boy."

Mrs. Horton, still holding Sunny Boy in her arms, smiled with wet dark eyes at Tim.

"She certainly was pretty," said Tim afterward to his mother. "Tall as Theresa, and young and dressed up nice and all. But she shook hands with me just as if I was a friend of hers. I guess all mothers are nice and friendly."

By this time a little crowd had gathered about the Hortons, for many of the guests at the hotel had heard that Sunny Boy was lost and they wanted to tell his father and mother how glad they were that he was safely found. Tim began to get decidedly restless.

"I got to go," he whispered to Mr. Horton. "Ma won't know what's keeping me. 'Sides I have to be up at five in the morning to cover my paper route."

"Olive," said Mr. Horton to his wife, "suppose you take the boy up. I want to have a little talk with Tim" (for Sunny of course had told them his name) "and we're going into the grill room where there won't be so many people. I guess we can have a bite to eat if we have had supper."

"And we had Welsh rabbit and coffee," Tim recounted to his admiring family later that night. "The grill room's just a restaurant. I'll bet that waiter didn't want me coming in there looking like a tramp, but Mr. Horton never let on I looked any different from the rest of 'em."

Sunny Boy and his mother went up in the elevator, and after they were in their room, while she undressed him, "for," she said, "I'm so glad to have my baby back I must undress him and put him to bed just as I used to when he was really a baby," he told her about the Harritys and how he had met Tim.

"We rode up and down in the subway, hunting for you," explained Mrs. Horton. "Daddy asked every guard, and I even asked the ticket sellers if they had seen a little boy in a blue suit. Then we thought you might have remembered the name of the hotel, and we hurried back here in case you should manage to get here before we did."

"Did you cry?" asked Sunny Boy, patting her cheek, as he lay in her lap.

"Yes, I did," admitted Mother softly. "Poor Daddy had a hard time of it. But, darling, we won't talk of it any more—you're all right and Mother is very happy. I'll lie down beside you here on the bed till you go to sleep." And going to sleep did not take long.

"Where's Tim?" asked Sunny Boy when he woke up the next morning.

He had slept later than usual, after his exciting day, and Mother was up and dressed and sewing fresh ruffles in her coat over by the window. Daddy was not in the room.

"Good morning, precious," Mrs. Horton greeted him. "You've had a fine long sleep. Daddy has been gone an hour—he had a telephone call before breakfast."

"Did Tim stay all night? Is he here now?" asked Sunny Boy, slipping out of bed and beginning to hunt for his socks and shoes. "Do I have to take a bath, Mother?"

"Yes indeed you do," said Mother. "We are going down town, you and I, on a very important shopping trip, and I want you to be as clean and as fresh as a rose when we start. And if you hurry, I'll tell you about Tim while you are eating your breakfast."

Sunny Boy hurried, and in less than half an hour he was sitting at the table in the big dining room eating breakfast with Mother, who had waited for him.

"Tell me about Tim," begged Sunny Boy when the waiter had brought him his orange and asked him how he felt; the waiter knew he had been lost.

"Well, Daddy had a long talk with Tim last night," said Mrs. Horton. "We wanted to reward him in some way for his kindness to you and his good sense in going about to find where you lived. But Tim wouldn't take any money. He said his mother wouldn't let him."

"Then can't Daddy 'ward him?" asked Sunny Boy disappointedly.

"Listen," said Mrs. Horton. "Daddy got Tim to tell about his family. His mother is a widow with six children, and, dear, she takes in washing. She was washing last night when you were there, clothes for her own children, after having done two big washes at other houses that day. Theresa, who is sixteen, works in a department store, and Tim sells papers before and after school, and sometimes, I am afraid, when he plays hooky. He can't leave school till he is at least fourteen and he is only thirteen now. Of course the other children are too young to help."

"Theresa can cook," announced Sunny Boy. "She made stew."

"Theresa does most everything," returned his mother. "But what she wants to do is to be a dressmaker. And Daddy has prevailed on Tim to let him send her to a trade school where she can learn to sew. After she has graduated, if she wishes, she can pay him back the money. Daddy had to arrange it that way because the Harritys are proud and independent."

"And Tim?" urged Sunny Boy, forgetting to eat his egg.

"Oh, Tim is to go to school, too," said Mrs. Horton. "Daddy knows a man who has a school for boys like Tim where they can work and pay for their education, and if Tim can have three or four years there he will be able to help his mother much more than if he got 'working papers' at fourteen and left school."

"Why didn't he go there before?" demanded Sunny Boy. "If he can pay for it himself, he wouldn't be too poor, would he, Mother?"

"Well, you see, he didn't know about this school," said Mrs. Horton. "And then you must remember that he has been helping his mother. Even the little he earned was sorely needed by Mrs. Harrity. So Daddy had to plan for her, too."

"So she won't have to wash?" suggested Sunny Boy eagerly.

"So she won't have to wash," assented Mrs. Horton. "She is to have an apartment rent-free in exchange for janitor work. A man does the heavier work and has four or five apartment houses to take care of, but they want some one to clean the halls, and so on. Tim said it was what his mother often planned. And then she wants to take in a boarder or two. I told Daddy I didn't see that she was having it any easier, but at least she will have a warm, comfortable home this winter. And Daddy is going to keep an eye on them this winter through New York friends. She must be willing to let us help her till her children are old enough."

Sunny Boy finished his breakfast rather soberly. He was learning that all little boys didn't have the many nice things he had. Marty and Thomas, for instance, had they had the kind of breakfast he had just had?

"And we're going shopping," Mother reminded him, as she led the way out of the dining room. Perhaps she guessed what he was thinking. "You see, Daddy did all this for you and for me, but we want to give the Harritys something, don't we?"

"Oh, yes!" Sunny Boy was all smiles. "Let's, Mother! But what shall we buy?"

"I thought I'd send something nice to Mrs. Harrity and Theresa, and you would choose something for each of the children," explained Mrs. Horton. "We'll go right out now and see what we can find."

When they reached the corner Mrs. Horton was confused for a moment. She couldn't remember whether to turn up or down to get to the particular shop she wanted.

"I'll find out," said Sunny Boy.

Before she could stop him, he had dashed out into the middle of the street and was speaking to the tall policeman who directed traffic from the center of the street. He was so tall that he had to bend down to hear what Sunny Boy was saying.

Mrs. Horton, on the curb, saw him laugh, then point up the street and, as Sunny Boy started back to her, the policeman blew his whistle and stopped the traffic till Sunny Boy was safely across.

"What made you do that?" demanded Mrs. Horton. "It's never safe to run out into the street like that. I didn't know you were even going."

"Daddy and I know that p'liceman," said Sunny Boy calmly. "He s'lutes us—sometimes. I asked him which way to go, and he showed me. That's why they stand in the middle of the street, Mother; to show people where to go."

"What did you say that made him laugh?" Mrs. Horton asked, as she and Sunny Boy started to walk in the direction the policeman had pointed. "You were so little, Sunny, and he was so tall, I don't see how you ever heard each other."

Sunny Boy was puzzled for a minute.

"Did he laugh?" he said. "Oh, yes, I 'member. I asked him please not to step on me. His feet are pretty big when you're close to him."

"And here is the store," smiled Mrs. Horton. "Your policeman knew where we wanted to go, didn't he? Begin now and think what you would want most if you were Tim Harrity."

CHAPTER XIV
JOE BROWN GOES BACK

S unny Boy thought about what Tim would like all the while Mrs. Horton was buying things for Mrs. Harrity. He wondered, too, why she bought such queer articles—sheets and towels and pillow cases.

"Because, precious," she explained when he asked her, "I know Mrs. Harrity will want to have things clean and comfortable in the new home. And she can not have two or three boarders unless she has bed and table linen. You're not a housekeeper, but she and I understand. And for her very own present, something just for her own use, I'm going to send her this pretty gray bathrobe and slippers."

"And Theresa?" said Sunny Boy, forgetting Tim for the moment.

"Theresa shall have regular shoes and stockings and also a pair of silk stockings and slippers to match," announced Mrs. Horton. "I know what it is to be poor and young and pretty and not have the right things to wear to a party. She can bring the slippers back if they're not the right size."

"How can she go to parties if they're poor?" questioned Sunny Boy curiously.

"Oh, poor people often have the best parties," said his mother. "They always manage to have a good time. And Theresa is going to school, you know, and there will be little affairs now and then to which she'll want to go. Anyway, Son, girls like to have pretty clothes if only to look at."

Sunny Boy didn't know much about girls' clothes, but he liked his mother's pretty dresses. He thought it was nice if Theresa could have some, too.

"I've thought ever so hard," he complained, "but I can't think of a thing to send Tim."

"Let me put on my thinking cap," mused Mrs. Horton. "Tim is thirteen, isn't he? Daddy will see that he has a new suit for school, but wouldn't you like to send him hockey skates? Boys with fathers and mothers and good homes have those things, but I'm sure Tim hasn't; he hasn't even had time to play very much. We'll get him skates, and then he can try for the hockey team at school."

Sunny Boy thought this a fine selection, and he and Mother went upstairs and chose a pair of skates.

"Now there's only Marty and Thomas and Rose and Jim," declared Sunny Boy, when the skates had been ordered and paid for.

Mrs. Horton laughed.

"I should say that was a great many," she said. "I don't see how you remember their names. Well, now let's see—Rose must have a new doll and a couple of pretty dresses I think; and for the boys suppose we say good warm school gloves and sweaters and a game apiece, so they won't think you and I choose too useful gifts?"

The gloves and sweaters were bought, and then Sunny Boy picked out three games he thought the boys would like and helped Mother decide about a doll for Rose and a pink dress and a blue one. Then they were through for the morning.

"We'll go back to the hotel for lunch," decided Mrs. Horton. "Daddy may come in. And I must write a note to Harriet this afternoon."

Mr. Horton was waiting for them, and he had great news.

"How would you like to go home day after to-morrow?" he asked.

"Home?" repeated Mrs. Horton. "Why, Harry!"

"Haven't you seen enough of New York?" Mr. Horton asked Sunny Boy, tilting up his chin.

"We-ll," hesitated Sunny, "I guess so. But I did want to see the stuffed birds."

"Stuffed birds?" echoed his father.

"I promised to take him over to the Museum of Natural History," Mrs. Horton explained. "But of course, Daddy, if you are ready to go, we are."

"Well, I'm through a week earlier than I expected," said Mr. Horton. "And if you can be ready by Friday, there's no reason why we should stay longer."

"I'm anxious to get Sunny Boy started in school," answered Mrs. Horton thoughtfully. "We'll wire Bessie to have Harriet open the house, and I have very little packing to do. Yes, we'll be ready easily by Friday."

Mr. Horton was consulting a time table.

"I'd like to go down to the station this afternoon," he said, "and see about reservations. The hotel will do it, of course, but I like to attend to such matters myself. Suppose you and Sunny Boy go with me and then go on to the Museum."

So after lunch Sunny Boy and his mother went over to the big Pennsylvania Station with Daddy and waited for him to get their tickets for Centronia.

"It's the biggest place," observed Sunny Boy. "And such lots and lots of people!"

"I dare say we could stand here all day, or a week for that matter, and never see a soul we knew," returned Mrs. Horton.

"Why Mother!" Sunny Boy almost shouted in his excitement, "there's somebody we know this minute—over there by that window. It's Joe Brown!"

"We'll go over and speak to him," said Mrs. Horton.

As they came up to the window they heard the ticket agent speaking to the boy.

"Seven sixty-five, one way to Centronia," said the agent.

"But I don't want a parlor car seat or nothing," protested Joe Brown.

"That doesn't count in a Pullman," retorted the agent. "Seven sixty-five one way, I tell you."

Joe Brown shuffled his shabby feet uneasily.

"How—how—how little do you have to be to get half-fare?" he blurted.

"A sight smaller than you are," snapped the agent. "Do you want a ticket or not?"

Joe Brown looked at the crumpled wad of dirty bills and loose change in his hand.

"I guess I won't take it just now," he mumbled, and turned away.

"Hello, Joe!" Sunny Boy pounced upon him gleefully, having waited till this minute only because his mother had held him back. "How are you?"

"Pretty well, thank you," answered Joe politely, flushing a little.

"Joe, do you want to go home?" asked Mrs. Horton gravely. "I overheard you talking with the ticket agent. Haven't you enough money?"

Joe Brown looked at her quickly, then away again.

"I would kinda like to go home," he admitted.

"Oh, Joe!" Mrs. Horton cried half impatiently, half laughing. "Come over here and sit down a minute. Now tell me truly. Did you run away, and do you want to go back?"

Joe sat down on one side of her, and Sunny Boy scrambled into the seat on the other side. He leaned over her shoulder to listen.

"Well, yes, I did run away," confessed Joe humbly. "That is, I meant to go see my Aunt Annabell, and write the folks from her house. But she had moved, honest she had; I couldn't locate her nowhere. And then I thought I'd get me a job and wear new clothes home. But New York isn't such an easy place to get along in. These don't look much like new clothes."

Mrs. Horton glanced at the shabby suit.

"But your mother, Joe?" she urged. "Haven't you written to her?"

"I sent her postals telling her not to worry," answered Joe.

"And now you want to go home?" asked Mrs. Horton.

Sunny Boy, watching the careless, slouching Joe, was surprised to see great tears come into his eyes suddenly. He tried to wipe them away with his coat sleeve.

"I want to go home!" he choked. "It's been an awful long time, and I'm so lonesome—and there's my mother!"

Sunny Boy's mother tucked a clean little white handkerchief into Joe's hand.

"Don't cry," she said kindly. "We'll see that you get home. Here comes Mr. Horton. He'll make it all right."

When Mr. Horton heard that Joe wanted to go home, he said it was the "easiest thing in the world."

"I'll get your ticket and see you on the train," he promised. "There's a local leaving in half an hour. You'll be in Centronia by eight o'clock to-night."

"But I haven't enough money," faltered Joe.

"I'll lend it to you," said Mr. Horton, just as he would speak to a business friend. "Then next week you come down to the office and we'll talk things over. How will that do?"

Joe said he guessed it was all right, and while he and Mr. Horton went off to buy the ticket, Mrs. Horton and Sunny Boy bought a bag of fruit and sandwiches for Joe to have on the train.

"He looks half starved," commented Mrs. Horton. "Won't his mother enjoy getting him a good meal!"

"When you going home?" Joe Brown asked, as they walked with him to the train gate. "Wish it was now."

"We're coming to-morrow," said Mrs. Horton, "Say good-bye to Joe, precious. He'll be home before you are."

Joe shook hands awkwardly with Sunny Boy and then with Mr. and Mrs. Horton.

"I sure am obliged to you," he said shyly.

They watched him pass through the gate and down the platform, and saw a brakeman point to the train he was to board. At the steps Joe turned again, and waved to them.

"I'm glad he's out of New York," declared Mr. Horton. "This city is no place for a friendless boy. And now you and Sunny Boy go on up to the Museum, and I'll see you at dinner."

Sunny Boy enjoyed another ride on top of his beloved bus, and then he and Mother spent a couple of busy and happy hours looking at the wonderful exhibits in the Museum of Natural History.

"Jack said to see the birds," Sunny insisted, for Jack, the bell-boy at the hotel, had his own ideas as to what was worth seeing in New York.

After the birds came the Eskimo cases, and after them, those given over to the American Indians. And then, quite by accident, Sunny Boy and his mother came to the exhibits of the marvelous gigantic creatures that were the animals of this world centuries ago.

"My goodness!" gasped Sunny Boy, startled, when he caught his first glimpse of a creature labeled with a long name that he couldn't hope to read. "What's that, Mother?"

"That's the way the animals used to look," said Mrs. Horton smiling. "You'd be surprised, wouldn't you, if when you went to take a walk some morning you saw this great thing coming over the field toward you?"

"I wouldn't want to see him," said Sunny Boy decidedly. "Are there more of 'em? Hurry up, Mother, and let's see this one in the corner."

"Now don't dream about any of them," said Mrs. Horton jokingly, as they went down the Museum steps.

"Course not," answered Sunny Boy stoutly. "I never dream—hardly any, I mean. And we're going home to-morrow, aren't we?"

CHAPTER XV
HOME AGAIN

The next morning Mrs. Horton did their packing and the trunk was sent early to the station. Sunny Boy was just as excited at the prospect of going home as he had been at the idea of the trip to New York.

"But what will you do all the time at home?" teased Jack the bell-boy, when Sunny Boy went to say good-bye to him.

"Oh, I'm going to school," announced Sunny Boy proudly. "All the children that I know go. Harriet's going to take me till I get used to it, and then Mother says p'haps I can go by myself."

"Would you like to live here?" Sunny Boy asked Mother, when they had found their comfortable seats in the train and it was almost time for it to start.

"Live in New York?" echoed Mrs. Horton thoughtfully. "No, I think not, precious. Though we have had a good time, haven't we?"

Sunny Boy nodded his head.

"I wouldn't like to live here all the time, either," he confided. "I'd rather live in our house."

The train ride was uneventful, and as they had taken an express, they were in Centronia by early afternoon. Aunt Bessie met them at the station.

"Well, well, honey-bunch," she greeted her nephew, hugging him, "I surely have missed you. What do you think of New York?"

"All right," said Sunny Boy, wriggling out of her arms. "Did the children get the post cards I sent them?"

"I think they did," admitted Aunt Bessie gravely. "Ruth Baker talks a great deal about her post-card album, I know. What is this I hear about you going to school?"

Aunt Bessie and Sunny Boy were seated in the tonneau of Mr. Horton's car which Aunt Bessie had driven down to meet him. Mrs. Horton was sitting in the front seat with Mr. Horton who was driving.

"I'm going to school!" beamed Sunny Boy. "Did Mother tell you? And then I can write in ink."

"That will be fine," said Aunt Bessie. "Here's the house, though, and there's Harriet standing on the step."

"Harriet! Harriet! I've come home," yelled Sunny Boy. "And I brought you something! Mother has it in the trunk!"

Harriet came down as the car drew up at the curb and tried to shake hands with Mrs. Horton, carry a suitcase for Mr. Horton and hug Sunny Boy all at once.

"Did you miss me?" demanded Sunny Boy, following her upstairs.

"Miss you? Well, I should say so!" declared Harriet, kissing him again. "Haven't I been up and dusted all your toys every time I came over to see that the house was all right? You'll find them all sitting up there in the playroom waiting for you."

Sunny Boy was very glad to be at home, and after he had inspected his toys he went out into the back yard and whistled for Ruth and Nelson. Ruth was not at home, but Nelson answered and had a hundred questions to ask about New York.

"Say, you remember the boy that took your new hat?" he suddenly reminded Sunny Boy. "Well, I know him. He lives back over in Oak Lane, near where Molly lives."

Molly was the colored woman who did Mrs. Baker's washing.

"Let's go over and get it from him," suggested Nelson. "He won't dare say a word. I'll tell Molly if he does and she'll tell his mother."

Sunny Boy thought it would be nice to have the hat back, so he said he would go with Nelson. After a short walk the boys reached the section where the colored people lived and turned down a street where Nelson said he had seen the colored boy who had taken Sunny's hat.

"There he is now!" shouted Nelson, pointing to a boy sitting on the curbstone.

The boy heard him, looked up and started to run. Sunny Boy and Nelson ran pell-mell after him. As the colored boy dodged round a truck in the street the hat fell off.

"Told you we'd get it!" boasted Nelson, picking it up and holding it triumphantly out to Sunny Boy. "That's the very one, isn't it?"

They carried it home, and Sunny Boy went to find Harriet.

"Got my hat, Harriet," he announced soberly. "Nelson helped me chase the boy that stole it. It fell off."

"Well, you don't seem very joyful over it," commented Harriet. "Where is it?"

Sunny Boy held out the hat silently.

It was spotted, and the brim was crushed, the ribbon band was slashed in several places, and the crown was hopelessly faded from the sun.

"He had it on," explained Sunny Boy. "Somehow, I don't feel much like wearing it any more."

Harriet pulled Sunny Boy down into her lap.

"For a lost hat, I'd consider that one still lost," she told him, laughing. "That boy must have been wearing it rather steady. Don't you care, Sunny, it isn't as if you needed it."

"No, 'tisn't as if I needed it," agreed Sunny Boy, picking up the dilapidated hat and going off to show it to his mother. "I have my new one. Only it's not new any more. But it looks better than this one, I think, a whole lot."

So, like the cat, his hat came back. And now if you want to read what happened to Sunny Boy next and what a busy time the next few weeks were for him, you will have to read the book about him called "SUNNY BOY IN SCHOOL AND OUT."

THE END

THE SUNNY BOY SERIES

By Ramy Allison White

Children, meet Sunny Boy, a little fellow with big eyes and an inquiring disposition, who finds the world a large and wonderful thing indeed. And somehow there is lots going on, when Sunny Boy is around. Perhaps he helps push! In the first book of this new series he has the finest time ever, with his Grandpa out in the country. He learns a lot and he helps a lot, in his small way. Then he has a glorious visit to the seashore, but this is in the next story. And there are still more adventures in other books. You will like Sunny Boy.

1. SUNNY BOY IN THE COUNTRY
2. SUNNY BOY AT THE SEASHORE
3. SUNNY BOY IN THE BIG CITY
4. SUNNY BOY IN SCHOOL AND OUT
5. SUNNY BOY AND HIS PLAYMATES
6. SUNNY BOY AND HIS GAMES
7. SUNNY BOY IN THE FAR WEST
8. SUNNY BOY ON THE OCEAN
9. SUNNY BOY WITH THE CIRCUS
10. SUNNY BOY AND HIS BIG DOG

GOOD STORIES FOR CHILDREN

(From four to nine years old)

THE KNEETIME ANIMAL STORIES

By RICHARD BARNUM

In all nursery literature animals have played a conspicuous part; and the reason is obvious, for nothing entertains a child more than the antics of an animal. These stories abound in amusing incidents such as children adore, and the characters are so full of life, so appealing to a child's imagination, that none will be satisfied until they have met all of their favorites—Squinty, Slicko, Mappo, and the rest.

1. Squinty, the Comical Pig.
2. Slicko, the Jumping Squirrel.
3. Mappo, the Merry Monkey.
4. Tum Tum, the Jolly Elephant.
5. Don, a Runaway Dog.
6. Dido, the Dancing Bear.
7. Blackie, a Lost Cat.
8. Flop Ear, the Funny Rabbit.
9. Tinkle, the Trick Pony.
10. Lightfoot, the Leaping Goat.
11. Chunky, the Happy Hippo.

12. Sharp Eyes, the Silver Fox.
13. Nero, the Circus Lion.
14. Tamba, the Tame Tiger.
15. Toto, the Rustling Beaver.
16. Shaggo, the Mighty Buffalo.
17. Winkie, the Wily Woodchuck.

Cloth, Large 12mo., Illustrated.

THE BOBBY BLAKE SERIES

BY FRANK A. WARNER

BOOKS FOR BOYS FROM EIGHT TO TWELVE YEARS OLD

True stories of life at a modern American boarding school. Bobby attends this institution of learning with his particular chum and the boys have no end of good times. The tales of outdoor life, especially the exciting times they have when engaged in sports against rival schools, are written in a manner so true, so realistic, that the reader, too, is bound to share with these boys their thrills and pleasures.

1. BOBBY BLAKE AT ROCKLEDGE SCHOOL.
2. BOBBY BLAKE AT BASS COVE.
3. BOBBY BLAKE ON A CRUISE.
4. BOBBY BLAKE AND HIS SCHOOL CHUMS.
5. BOBBY BLAKE AT SNOWTOP CAMP.
6. BOBBY BLAKE ON THE SCHOOL NINE.
7. BOBBY BLAKE ON A RANCH.
8. BOBBY BLAKE ON AN AUTO TOUR.
9. BOBBY BLAKE ON THE SCHOOL ELEVEN.
10. BOBBY BLAKE ON A PLANTATION.
11. BOBBY BLAKE IN THE FROZEN NORTH.
12. BOBBY BLAKE ON MYSTERY MOUNTAIN.

Famous Americans For
Young Readers

"Life Stories with the Charm of Fiction"

"This new series is timely. As an urgent civic need, our schools should be vivified more by the spirit of the founders and builders of the Republic."

WALTER E. RANGER,

Commissioner of Education, Rhode Island.

"I regard the series one of rare usefulness for young readers, and trust it will become a formidable rival for much of the fiction now in circulation among the young."

JOHNSON BRIGHAM, State Librarian, Iowa.

Titles Ready

"GEORGE WASHINGTON"   Joseph Walker

"JOHN PAUL JONES"   Chelsea C. Fraser

"BENJAMIN FRANKLIN"   Clara Tree Major

"DAVID CROCKETT"   Jane Corby

"THOMAS JEFFERSON"   Gene Stone

"ABRAHAM LINCOLN"   J. Walker McSpadden

"ROBERT FULTON"   Inez N. McFee

"THOMAS A. EDISON"   Inez N. McFee

"HARRIET BEECHER STOWE"   Ruth Brown MacArthur

"MARY LYON"   H. Oxley Stengel

"THEODORE ROOSEVELT"   J. Walker McSpadden

Illustrated. Size 5-1/8 x 7-5/8. Cloth.

OTHER VOLUMES IN PREPARATION

CPSIA information can be obtained
at www.ICGtesting.com
Printed in the USA
LVHW041803190621
690653LV00005B/560

9 781006 959158